Bad Mom
rents a man

· · · · · ① · · · · ·

Mother's Day

sydney strand

"Sydney"

treat books
www.treatbooks.com

Treat Books
www.treatbooks.com

Cover Image: Shutterstock/Prosyanyk Martyna
Cover Design: Treat Books

Printed in the United States of America

Strand, Sydney
Bad Mom Rents a Man: Mother's Day
Sydney Strand – 1st Edition
ISBN: 978-0-9912205-4-0 (Print)
ISBN: 978-0-9912205-3-3 (eBook)
1. Single mothers—Fiction.
2. Working mothers—Fiction.

Dedication

To my mom. Always.

And to all single moms, past, present, and future.
You are *awesome*.

Where to Find Sydney

Books by sydneystrand

His Favorite Regret

His Favorite Inconvenience

Bad Mom Rents a Man: Mother's Day (Book 1)

Places to find sydneystrand

www.sydneystrand.com

www.facebook.com/sydney.strand

www.instagram.com/sydneystrand

www.pinterest.com/sydneystrand

Ways to talk to sydneystrand

sydneystrandbooks@gmail.com

Letter to My Reader

Welcome to the start of a new series: *Bad Mom Rents a Man*.
This is Book 1, the Mother's Day edition.

I enjoy watching a romance unfold. I love the ebb and flow,
the ups and downs, the butterflies and the fights. When love
is growing, it's oh-so-fun to watch (and in this case, read!).

That's why this series exists: to see the romance grow. To
watch it retreat. To see strangers become friends. To see
friends become best friends. To see best friends… Well, I
don't want to ruin anything.

Who are our two strangers? There's Maggie Weston, a
children's party planner and overall happy human who is
dealing with the guilt single motherhood has branded her
with. And then there's Augustus Sloane, an entomologist,
who is a straight-shooter who is easy on the eyes but
sometimes hard to take.

This series chronicles their adventures in renting and being
rented. These stories are meant to be fun and sweet and a
little sexy. They take place in and around a quaint New
Hampshire college town, much like the town I live in. I love
college towns, and I think there's something joyous and
invigorating when living in one.

While you may not know how their story ends by the end of
Book 1, Maggie and Augustus's story is worth sticking
around for. Bit by crazy bit…

sydney strand

Bad
(*adjective*)

36 Definitions

1. not good

. . .

4. inadequate

. . .

19. disreputable

. . .

22. unsuitable

. . .

26. misbehaving

. . .

36. outstandingly excellent (Slang)

Chapter One

IT WAS 10:32 P.M. AND A SCHOOL NIGHT, and eight-year-old Roxie Riveter Weston had an iPad in her smeared from her inner eye to her temple.

She sat on a yellow resin chair in the Workout World waiting area, a blue sucker in her mouth and a bedazzled yet threadbare Smurfette across her too-big shirt.

To the outside observer, she either wanted to be Smurfette or she wanted to be Honey Boo Boo.

Roxie's mother Magdalene—or Maggie, if you wanted her to answer—had learned a long time ago that each day with a child was filled with two kinds of battles: those that won the war, and those that did not.

Blue eye shadow did not win the war.

And so the blue eye shadow stayed.

Maggie knew that what she saw as just a bump in the road was someone else's cliff edge. Those kind of people would never get Maggie.

So those kind of people could suck it.

Sweat dripped down Maggie's neck. She wiped it away with her towel, the screen on her treadmill telling her she had two more minutes left before her five miles were done and over. Two more minutes until she could climb off this thing and walk across the street, Roxie's hand in hers. Scrub her down, put her in her footie pajamas, and harmonize *Doe, a deer, a female deer,* before turning off Roxie's light and getting back to work.

She wouldn't be getting to bed anytime soon, either. Her brain was racing almost as fast as her Nikes:

E-mail Jessa.
Write a new blog post.
Find Roxie's headbands.
Find the unicorn.
Set alarm for 4 a.m.

She pressed the plus sign on the treadmill's dashboard. She went from a punishing 9 minutes per mile to a crazy-ass 6 minutes per mile for her last 60 seconds. She pushed her earbuds in even deeper and sang along.

Sixty seconds of pain, and then this part of the day would be done.

And then she could go to sleep, rest her brain for a few hours, and start the mad scramble on the squeaky hamster wheel all over again.

The machine beeped at the exact moment her cellphone told her she had a text. Joan Jett kept singing and Maggie read her message:

*I'm thinking pajama sets. Each girl's name
embroidered on the front. Thoughts?*

Maggie had thoughts all right. She tapped back:

*Three days left. Embroidery turnaround is seven days,
even with money thrown at it. Unless you know a
bored grandma? =o)*

Being a party planner who specialized in children's
parties was her dream job. Except for these moments,
when she was getting texts at 11 p.m. about last-minute
brainstorms. That's when this job got *not* so dreamy.

Speaking of dreamy...time for Rox to visit Sleepy
Town. Maggie looked across the room at her daughter,
still seated where she had left her forty-five minutes
ago.

Her daughter was looking at her. Then the little smart
ass dropped her head back, closed her eyes, and gave an
exaggerated performance of snoring. Maggie felt her
face split into a huge smile.

She loved that smart ass so, so much.

Maggie started pushing the minus sign on the
treadmill, slowing her speed, her forty-five minutes
done and over for the night.

Tomorrow, there'd be another forty-five minutes.

The night after that, too. She wouldn't be on a
treadmill, though, because they were traveling to the
middle of nowhere. It would just be the two of them,
dirt roads, and maybe the occasional moose sighting. It
was a no-stress, no-frills way to spend Mother's Day

Weekend, and Maggie couldn't wait for it to begin.

Because right now, jogging and the rare opportunity to get away helped combat the stress that threatened to overwhelm her if she wasn't careful.

"I can't believe someone would bring their child here this time of night."

The words were said too loudly, and Maggie was the only person close enough to hear them.

Maggie obliged. If this person wanted to talk to her, Maggie would help her out.

That person was a girl wearing an NHU shirt and on the elliptical next to Maggie's treadmill. In a voice that continued to be passive aggressively loud, she added, "She should be shot and her kid should be taken away."

The girl was talking to another girl on the elliptical next to her, a girl who had about ten studs lining the edge of her ear and blonde hair with purple tips twisted into a teeny-tiny bun on top of her head. They both looked like they were nineteen, maybe twenty.

Their hips looked like they were nineteen, maybe twenty inches.

They were definitely college students. Maggie had never gone to college, but here she was, in Maple Woods, New Hampshire, home of the state's largest university.

Maple Woods had an excellent K-12 school system. And, apparently, college students who were eager to share their naive, dumbass opinions.

Maggie pulled antibacterial wipes from the treadmill's drink holder, which she had placed there before her run, and wiped away every spot that her sweat had hit and dripped down.

She bet these two girls would take off, sweat slimed everywhere, as soon as they were done. Proving yet again that a person didn't need college to be a better human being.

Across the small gym space, Roxie pulled off her headphones and called out, "Mom, I gotta pee. Should I go here or at home?"

"Home. We'll get there in a minute, LaLa."

The two girls stopped talking and were now unnaturally busy with the controls on their ellipticals. They must not have realized Maggie could hear them, even with the earbuds in.

She'd love to tell these girls that she had made Roxie take a nap after school. She'd love to let them know she couldn't get here any sooner because she had to find a new bakery to bake a perfume-shaped cake in in time for Jamison James's sixth birthday party. She'd love to tell them she had to unpack six boxes in the middle of being a mom and a party planner in order to find clean clothes for Roxie. She'd then love to tell them she had to find time and energy to make dinner for her kid.

It had been microwaved mac and cheese, but still. The minutes had added up until it was 9:30.

Maggie would love to tell these two girls that her only time to work out was at night, and how exercise was the only way to manage the stress that gave her stomach cramps and her head migraines. Running was the only thing that helped. She owned exercise tapes, everything from yoga to Pilates to kickboxing, but nothing worked as well as running.

And running meant she didn't have to worry about disturbing her neighbors who lived next to her and under her in her third-story walk-up.

Maggie would love to tell these two girls that she had just moved to town. That she didn't know or trust anyone well enough to leave her kid with.

She'd love to tell them a little blue eye shadow wouldn't kill a person.

But Maggie wasn't one to make excuses or to defend her life, at least not to strangers.

(Except her mother. When it came to Abigail Weston, Maggie was a fucking mess.)

But these girls weren't anything like Abigail Weston.

But Maggie was. At least in backbone, which was the best part of Abigail Weston.

Maggie stepped off her treadmill and planted herself in front of the ellipticals. She waited for eye contact. And when she got it, she said, "Hi there."

The girls didn't look away, but they didn't say anything, either.

"I just wanted to say that yes, I'm The Bad Mom." She gave a smile that she hoped was just as sickly sweet as her words. She turned to go, her words shared, her stomach happy about it. But then she turned back.

And because she wasn't perfect, she added, "Isn't it finals next week? I hope that doesn't make you bad students being here bullying strangers instead of studying."

Maggie turned and made her way to her daughter. And standing there with her blue eye shadow and her big smile was the biggest reason Maggie was who she was--and who she very much longed to be.

Chapter Two

THE NEXT MORNING, Maggie was seated at her kitchen table at 3:55 a.m. She had to mock up the cupcake toppers for Jamison James's sixth birthday, which fell on Mother's Day. But money was money. And they always needed money.

But planning this party had been a challenge. Jamison's mother was a Pinterest mother. Meaning Maggie's in-box was filled with Pinterested food, Pinterested decorations, and Pinterested party favors. And so Maggie was there to tell her what was practical (a hotel suite as the venue) and what was bone-headed (Chanel No. 5 as a party favor).

Maggie took a sip of her half-caf Breakfast Blend. She shouldn't even have that much caffeine—it hurt her stomach—but she needed a kickstart to her day. She hadn't gone to bed until 2 a.m. because she had been designing the banner for Jamie's Pajamas and Perfumery Party.

A little tummy ache, though, was better than a sleepy brain that got nothing done. And so Maggie nursed her meagerly caffeinated cup of coffee and took a minute to check emails.

Her eyes came to a screeching halt when she saw Abigail Weston's email

It was labeled *Read Now.*

Oh, hell and shit, Maggie cursed to herself.

Read Now it taunted.

No. No, she didn't want to read it now.

Instead, she moved on to the next email, the one from Jessa James labeled "Coffee beans to clear their noses!" It had been sent an hour ago, meaning that Jessa was up, too.

She would probably send ten more emails, even though they had an 8 a.m. phone call scheduled. And a 3:00 walk-thru at the venue.

Was all of this worth $300?

She is your way to drum up business in Maple Woods, Maggie reminded herself. *You'll get to know all the other mommies with too much money on their hands. And then they'll hire you and give you some of that money.*

Maggie blew out a hot, coffee-scented sigh. "Three hundred bucks, Maggie. Not the best money, but she knows people who know people. All insane like her, throwing money at you to give their kids memories."

And three hundred bucks would be appreciated. Her nest egg had taken a hit from paying first, last, and security, not to mention renting a truck and starting up utilities again. And with Roxie majorly growth spurting, they could comfortably buy more shirts that wouldn't show Roxie's belly or expose her wrist bones.

Maggie opened Jessa's email.
But she ignored her mother's.

Chapter Three

SOME KIDS ATE BANANAS AT BREAKFAST.
Roxie ate a green chile tamale like a banana at breakfast, still partially wrapped in its corn husk. She wore a blue dress, blue Mary Janes, and a blue Smurf backpack with a temperamental zipper. Roxie had bought it for two dollars at a yard sale, though, not Maggie. Maggie believed in cheap, but she drew the line at defective products she didn't have time to fix.

Roxie, however, never drew the line when it came to her beloved Smurfs.

Maggie dug through a box piled on top of two other boxes. "Are you sure you packed your headbands in here?"

"I put it in a box called 'stuff.'"

Maggie gritted her teeth. It had been a good day so far. She didn't want to mess with that. "LaLa, you wrote 'stuff' on every box. Which 'stuff' has your headbands in it?"

Roxie chowed on the tamale, shrugging. "Don't remember."

Maggie clenched her teeth, and looked inside the top box of a stack piled three high. "Well, this box of 'stuff' has puzzles and paint brushes."

"It won't be there."

"How do you know that?"

"Those are the P's."

"Of course they are," Maggie said under her breath. She stepped away from the box and washed her hands. There was soap but no towel. She hadn't found the towels yet.

She wiped her hands on her leggings and walked to her daughter, who had a strand of curly brown hair bouncing over one eye. Maggie touched the strand, still loose because they couldn't find the headbands.

Roxie ducked and scowled.

Maggie didn't do eight-year-old attitude. So she scowled right back and reached out once again, this time succeeding in shoving the hair behind Roxie's ear. "Watch it, Little Me. It's too early in the morning to be a little bum bum."

"I'm not a bum bum," she said, her eyes defiant, her lips a tight line. "Don't call me that."

"Everyone has it in them to be a bum bum. Today is just your day." Maggie grabbed her keys and they both walked out into the hallway, a scowl on her kid's face but at least she was moving.

Small battles. Small wins. They built up so that the losses wouldn't be so hard to take.

They started the trek down, their feet echoing against the metal stairs, the smell of beer strong. The apartment had been a last-minute choice. As in three days ago, Maggie found it on Craigslist, came to look at it, and then signed the lease.

When a decision had to be made, she had no problem making it. Even if it was a bad decision. But a bad decision sometimes had to be made in order to get out of a worse situation. And that's what Oceanview and its rapidly deteriorating schools and escalating crime rate had forced Maggie to do.

She hadn't had the $2500 a month that would've gotten her a house in a family-friendly neighborhood. The town was just too desirable for anyone on a budget to rent a *real* house. Instead, she had found an apartment for $800 a month and was now surrounded by college students who liked their beer.

But the college had finals next week, graduation on Friday, and then the town had two months of silence.

She could put up with beer smells for a week. Maggie focused on the fact that she would have the summer to find something better.

And to trade in her bad decision for a better one.

Out on the pavement, the air was still crispy. Maggie checked her cell phone. 7:55 a.m. The school had told her the bus would be by at 8:00. She put her phone away and walked to the curb.

She worked real hard at ignoring the smell of coffee coming from The Coffee Pot, coffee that smelled deliciously full of caffeine. But she could only handle one cup a day, barely caffeinated, and even that still made her sick.

Stupid sensitive stomach.

Snippets of conversation filled the early morning air.

"I haven't gone to class all semester."

"Dude. You going to pass?"

Then other voices came in, louder ones. Heated ones.

"I can't believe my dean isn't backing me up."

"Did you grade to the syllabus?"

"The syllabus is a suggestion. That's why you include 'This syllabus is subject to change.'"

"Then he has to back you up."

"Not if he's a fucker."

Maggie turned her head to hide her sudden smile. Sounded like the professors weren't the polite intellectuals she thought they'd be.

One man in a gray fleece jacket, coffee in hand, peeled himself away from a small knot of three women. She'd overheard their group talking about a field trip to D.C.

"Are you waiting for the school bus?" he asked, aviators shielding his eyes, a British accent shaping his words.

A bit of Maggie's stomach dropped. She loved a guy with an accent. "Yes, we are. Are we in the right spot?"

"Right spot, wrong time. The bus came ten minutes ago."

Maggie's stomachache grew worse. She rubbed the skin around her waistband and pulled her phone from her jacket pocket. She checked the time again. It was 7:57. "But it's not eight yet."

"This bus comes at 7:45."

Maggie groaned. She realized it must've been a loud groan when the conversations around her got quiet or stopped altogether.

She didn't have time to taxi Roxie into school today.

13

Not with her eight o'clock check-in with Jessa James and then her ten o'clock back in Oceanview with her long-standing Friday appointment.

"Did Denise in the front office tell you it was at eight?" the man asked. When he tilted his head, the day's morning sun caught his cheekbones, creating stark shadows that only emphasized how good-looking his face was. "She sometimes confuses the bus numbers."

Maggie didn't know who she had spoken to on the phone, and right now, she had to stop thinking about *stark shadows*. She had to concentrate on getting her kid to school, putting in a full day to bring in money, and unpacking just enough to find towels and headbands.

She gave a quick glance at Roxie, who was humming and dancing to some song that only she could hear, her hair in her face. *Where the hell are her headbands?* "I don't remember who I talked to. I just know that no bus is still no bus."

The man gave a small smile. "That is true."

Maggie liked this guy's company. But that didn't mean anything. She didn't have time for a full-time guy or a relationship that had to be fed and watered and cared for.

"Well, thanks," she said, her mind already moving on. It got busy crunching numbers and different plans of action.

The man frowned. Probably at her tone. She was an expert at pushing away guys that she didn't have time for.

"Any time," he said, polite but distant.

He started back to the group of women he had left.

The three of them were still watching Maggie, small frowns on their faces.

Oh, ladies. I will not be any competition to you at all. She called out to the guy's retreating back, "Thank you for everything. I'm being a grump, but I swear this isn't my natural state."

He turned back to her, the frown dropping off his face. "I understand completely. Don't even think twice about it. We've all been there."

Well hell. He didn't have to be so nice about it. That made her like him even more. "Thanks…?"

"Noah Fisher."

"Thank you Fisher, Noah Fisher."

He grinned. "You did that because of my accent."

"Yes, I did." Maggie was starting to like this guy and his accent. Anyone who got a simple *Bond, James Bond* reference was worth her momentary attention.

"See you around…?"

"Weston. Maggie Weston."

He lowered his aviators and gave her a quick wink before returning to his group. A group who was now looking at her like unwanted competition.

Oh relax ladies. He's safe from me.

I'm too busy being Bad Mom, missing the bus on her child's first day of school.

"We missed the bus?"

Maggie looked down to see Roxie's eyes huge and concerned. Two green eyes, perfectly matched. Beautiful eyes that saw the world in a way Maggie no longer did.

And that's why she didn't want to fuck up her relationship with her LaLa. She was the best thing that had ever happened to Maggie.

She put an arm around her daughter's shoulders. "I'm going to have to take you today. Sorry about that, Rox." She put her mouth against her daughter's ear, keeping her voice low. "I know how much you were looking forward to meeting the other kids on the bus."

She felt Roxie's shoulders move up and down. "That's okay."

"No, it's not." She lowered her voice even more. "I'll try harder." And she wasn't talking about a missed bus due to a wrong bus schedule. She was talking about an eight-year-old yawning at the gym at 11 p.m. She was talking about sleeping on a bare mattress because the sheets were hiding in some unopened box.

She was talking about having only one parent in a world that promoted two.

And as Maggie stood there thinking how much she sucked, Roxie turned and gave her a hug. The hard, no reservations kind that only a kid under the age of twelve knew how to give.

Chapter Four

MAGGIE'S CELLPHONE VIBRATED against the laminate of the counter, where it sat front and center for client calls and Roxie Emergencies. She picked it up, still chewing a chocolate donut hole, when part of the donut fell onto her black yoga pants. *This* was why she wore black. And the yoga pants? *They* were why she could eat donut holes from the day-old section at The Store Basket.

She started picking up chocolate crumbs, which made her answer without looking at the number first. Her bad. Her big, big bad.

"Maggie Weston speaking."

"Your mother speaking," said the voice on the other end.

Maggie clenched up, from the joints in her toes to the place where her hair attached to her scalp.

Shit!

"Hey there, stranger." Maggie winced as soon as the

word *stranger* came out. It wasn't because it wasn't true. It had been six months, after all, since she had last spoken to her mother. Right after the excruciating conversation in which Abigail Weston laid into her for allowing Roxie to wear lipstick and a tiara in her class picture.

Maggie had explained it had been lipgloss and every child in Mrs. Woodley's second grade class had gotten to choose the hat of their choice for the "fun" picture.

But Abigail Weston of Key West, Florida, did not want to hear any of it. Not when she thought the only thing Roxie Riveter Weston should be wearing was a white button-up shirt with some exclusive prep school crest on the front left pocket.

Since that lovely conversation, Maggie hadn't reached out to her mother.

And her mother hadn't reached out to her.

So…yeah. *Stranger* wasn't too far off the mark.

"I know you're busy so I'll get right down to it." Her mother was holding a grudge. Maggie could hear it in the way she spoke—clipped and emotionless. "I'll be in New Hampshire Saturday and Sunday."

"Next week?"

"Tomorrow."

Maggie clicked through computer screens, trying to find the right kind of printable for the perfume bottles that would be given to each and every little girl at Jamison James's sixth birthday party.

And then it sank in.

Tomorrow.

"You're coming to New Hampshire. Tomorrow." Maggie couldn't wrap her mind around this new information. This new, unwelcome information.

"Yes, Magdalene. I hope that's not going to be too much trouble for you?"

The full name already? Awesomeness. "No trouble, Mom. Just clarifying."

"And?"

"And..." She didn't know what her mother was after. There were so many things that pissed her mother off, which meant she never knew which one to go after. Which was a lot of the reason why Maggie was always on the outs with Abigail. And why she lived 2,000 miles away from her in New Hampshire.

"This weekend," Maggie clarified. "Mother's Day Weekend?"

"I have a meeting with The Montgomery to use my stemware. The Magdalene collection, funnily enough."

Oh so funny.

Maggie picked up a donut hole and shoved it in her mouth.

Funny that her mother, a tableware designer for thirty-five years, would name Maggie after a wine flute. A cute, innocent, sweet baby. Red ringlets and unmatched eyes and a voice that screamed every time the baby pissed in her diaper.

Yeah. That kind of baby had etched crystal with a price point starting at $225 written *all* over it.

"They've offered me their best suite," her mother was saying. "Actually, their entire top floor. And I wanted you to come and, of course, to bring Anne with you."

Maggie's hands curled until her fingernails impaled her flesh and made the nerves there burn in pain. "The name on her birth certificate is Roxie, not Roxanne."

"A nickname is not a name. Anne is a name. So much classier, and less like a hooker."

Wow. If Condescension and Judgment were an Olympic event, her mother would be stooped over by all the gold medals she would have on her neck.

Which Maggie hoped would choke her. Not to death just…to silence.

That thought made Maggie snap out of her thoughts. When had she started contemplating matricide?

Again?

Two thousand miles and six months of radio silence had totally not given her enough time to create a force field between her and her mother.

Abigail Weston still had the power to rip her heart and shred her feelings.

The chimes from the college's clock tower snapped Maggie back to the here and now. She realized that her mother hadn't said anything and she hadn't said anything, either. Maggie knew that Abigail wouldn't go first. So she did. "That took an awful turn, didn't it?"

"Yes." The word was clipped, and Maggie wasn't sure if her mom would say anything else.

Maggie prepared herself for the click on the other end. It wouldn't be the first time her mother had hung up on her.

"I was hoping that we could talk to each other like sane adults," her mother finally sighed. "That hope, I suppose, is not going to come true."

And then the silence started up again.

"Maybe next year," Maggie said.

"Talk to each other like sane adults?" her mother asked.

"No!" Wow. Her mom was all set to create a self-pity-party. Maggie was not going to get dragged into that. "I mean spending Mother's Day together."

"Oh." Then there was nothing. Just the sound of wind going over her mother's mouthpiece. Maggie could almost see the afternoon storm that was brewing as Abigail Weston sat out on her balcony, looking at her peek-a-boo view of the Atlantic. "The thing is, Maggie, your sisters will be in town."

Her sisters. Younger versions of her mother. Mortal enemies to her. *Yay.* "I have plans with Roxie."

"I'll pay the cancellation fees, Magdalene."

"There are no—" Maggie stopped herself. She had no reason to tell Abigail that it was a friend's cabin. That was ammunition Abigail would use to blow holes through her plans.

"Your sisters are bringing their children. Peyton will be there with Braden and Grayson, and Lauren will be there with Hayden and Jackson."

Oh goody. The Spawn would be there. Just hearing all those N's in one breath triggered the start of a headache behind Maggie's right eye. She dug at it with the heel of her hand. "Husbands too, I take it?"

"Of course. That's what women who are married do. They bring their husbands."

Maggie ignored what wasn't said but had been implied: *Women who are not married bring their nothings, like you.*

What she had was her child, and so Maggie started to focus on what she knew Roxie would want. Roxie would love to see her cousins. The last time she had seen them had been when she was three-years-old, and the four

21

young N's had worked together to bury her from her neck to her toes on some beach in Florida.

Roxie had selective memory, though. She didn't remember the way Peyton's boys had kept terrorizing her with crabs or how Lauren's girls had kept running away, keeping just out of Roxie's chubby-armed reach.

The kids were shits, but maybe five years had tamed them. *Maybe* was an awfully nebulous word, though. "We've had these plans for six months, Mom. I can't really change the game plan now."

Silence greeted her, and this one could have given the gap in the Grand Canyon a run for its money.

"I need you to listen, could you do that?" In one question, Abigail made Maggie feel like she was a kid again. And that Mommy knew best.

"Yes." Maggie couldn't help it. She sounded like a mouse. She could go toe to toe with just about anyone, but when it came to her mother in her forty-year-old pale blue Chanel suit and omnipresent costume pearls that were scuffed and ugly but had come from Joan Crawford's own personal collection, Maggie felt every inch of the woman her mother thought she was: a single mom scraping by.

Which wasn't that far from the truth.

"I'll be in New Hampshire tomorrow morning until Sunday evening. As will your sisters and their children and their significant others. I hope that you will be there with Anne and Ian."

There was that Anne again. And…Ian? "Ian?"

There was silence. Then: "That was his name. I know it is. I wrote it down and it's here in front of me, so don't tell me it wasn't."

Maggie didn't even know what her mom was getting in a tizzy over. "Who?"

A big, drawn-out, exasperated sigh traveled 2,000 miles over cell phone towers. "He's the man you became engaged to over Christmas, Magdalene."

Oh shit and hell.

"Is it already over? Did you and your strong personality scare off another man?"

"My strong personality?" She parroted the words to buy her time to think.

Dammit!

She had thrown out "Ian" to her mother on their obligatory Christmas call because it had shut her up.

That was the call that had created the six-month silence.

But a lot could happen in six months. Maggie opened her mouth to tell her mother exactly what had happened to poor, dear Ian.

Go with black bear mauling or lobster boat accident?

"Don't play surprised," her mother said. "You do realize, don't you, that you're role-modeling to your daughter that men are unnecessary?" Something like a pent-up breath sounded through the receiver. "I worry about you two. I worry so, so much."

Maggie used to feel guilty when her mother would say things like this to her. But being a mom now, she knew what it was like to worry for your child.

It was part of the job.

She got ready to tell her mother yet one more time that she had prior plans.

But then her eyes fell on the box she had opened earlier.

Puzzles and paintbrushes.

Things Roxie used by herself. Because in Oceanview, they hadn't lived close enough to anyone to have play dates.

Here in Maple Woods, Rox would probably be on her own for a while. At least until friends were made. Friends that could be so hard to make with only one more month of school left.

Maggie thought about the one-room cabin she was borrowing for the weekend. Small, but right on the water, a fire pit and kayaks steps away from the front door.

She had a choice to make.

Choice 1: Go to the cabin. Have fun with her daughter. Work on Jessa James's last-minute party details at the McDonald's that was half an hour from the cabin. Roxie would come with her each day, a strawberry shake in front of her, pouting as her mother took too long to get back to the cabin.

Choice 2: Go to The Montgomery. Let her daughter have fun or not have fun with her cousins. Let her daughter see her grandma for the first time in two years. Work on the James party on the hotel's WiFi while her daughter played and visited and smiled.

Maggie stopped going through choices as she tuned back in to the sixty-year-old woman still talking. "The room will be free. As will the Mother's Day Brunch, which is being prepared by a world-class chef. I've already booked massages, too, for all of the adults."

And because her mother didn't know when to stop: "You sound like you need one, Magdalene. Maybe even two."

One more thought entered Maggie's head:

Choice 3: The same as Choice Two, but with Free Shit.

Free shit is *free shit*, she told herself.

"Okay," she said.

"Okay?"

"I'll be there."

"Wonderful!" The joy in Abigail's voice did a funny thing to Maggie's heart. It made her remember that yes, she did love her mother.

Her infuriating, judgmental mother.

"And Ian?" she asked. "Will he be there too? Or will he be conveniently busy?"

Maggie's joyful heart returned to its normal size, deflated by her mother's low opinion of her. The judgment in Abigail's tone clawed at Maggie's nerves. She was tired, so tired. For once, Maggie wanted to smack people in the face with the fact that she was a good woman and a good mom who was making the most out of her life.

But to Abigail Weston, a good woman needed a good man.

And so Maggie found herself saying, "Ian will be there."

 *Chapter Five*

SHE ENDED THE CALL and put the phone next to her coffee mug. She straightened the mug, and then the phone, and then the mug again.

She had to come up with an "Ian" by tomorrow.

Shit and hell, and hell and shit.

Even as she face-palmed, Maggie let out a little pig snort as she remembered the exact moment she'd pulled "Ian" out of her butt. Her mother had just spent thirty minutes with no pauses going on about Peyton's and Lauren's husbands. They were a yacht company owner and a restaurateur, men who gave Abigail's two oldest daughters homes that had flat-screen TVs above outdoor fireplaces and granite countertops in the kids' baths.

The message was crystal clear: Her sisters were living the life, and when was Maggie going to get the clue and join them? Or, as Abigail put it, "I can't stop worrying about you. I go to sleep worried and I wake up worried."

And that's when "Ian" had materialized. Not because of an untapped desire for an "Ian," but because Maggie had to feel, for once, like she wasn't living a life of being a constant disappointment to her mother.

"You don't have to worry. I have a great man in my life," she had told her mom.

"You do?"

If Maggie had ever wondered how disbelief mingled with hope sounded like, she no longer needed to. "Yes. I do."

"Is it serious?" There was that hope, with less disbelief.

Maggie knew she had to answer only one way if this lie was to stick: "Yes."

"Oh my God, Magdalene! This is fantastic! Is he going to adopt Anne?"

Whoa. The happy trot Maggie had been enjoying with this nice, harmless lie had turned into a full-out gallop, her stomach jamming into the pummel, the reins out of reach as it turned into something with wild eyes and snapping teeth.

"We hav-haven't discussed that."

"Well, you should. Sooner rather than later. Is there a date at least?"

A date? No, there had been no date because there was no "Ian."

"Is it a church wedding at least?" her mother asked impatiently. "Please tell me you're doing something traditional for once in your...interesting...life."

Shit. Maggie scrambled for an answer while Abigail discussed March being the best month, of course, for an outdoor reception. That's when Key West was cool and

27

pleasant and the alligators weren't so hungry.

Maggie had added that last part. Her mother hadn't been amused.

Distant thunder crackling through the air and raindrops pounding the ground brought Maggie back to the present, her phone on its rainstorm setting. It was one small detail she had chosen to help alleviate the constant, unrelenting stress in her life.

Which had now been made worse with "Ian."

Maggie turned off the alarm and went to a box over by the couch, a lumpy pull-out that also acted as her bed. It had been a good couch in her Oceanview family room. But as a bed in her smaller Maple Woods apartment, it reminded her that she was thirty-four with a thirty-four-year-old's back.

From the box, she pulled out what she needed and smiled.

Her 10 a.m. client was going to love it.

"YOU ARE MAGICAL."

An older lady in a kitty cat sweatshirt and turquoise fanny pack came to stand next to Maggie, a clear pink plastic tea cup of sparkling pink cider in her arthritic hand. "How did you know Bella loves unicorns?"

"Four-year-olds the world over love unicorns, Mrs. Ram." Maggie piped another pink layer of icing on a teeny tiny cupcake. The unicorn would get this cupcake. The other four cupcakes had gone to Bear Bear, Hippo Hippo, Cat Cat, and Bella.

Bella loved stuffed animals, that was for sure. Roxie? Not so much. She hadn't even taken the tags off the unicorn when Grand had sent it to her for Christmas. She'd looked at it, scowled, tossed it on the couch and then never put it away.

Maggie had put it away—right into the re-gifting box in the closet.

"I'm going to call you…" The four-year old in the pink tutu, pink headband and pink wand paused.

Maggie offered, "Unicorn Unicorn?"

The little girl scowled. "That's dumb."

Maggie didn't expect anyone to correct Bella. Spoiled little girls usually weren't owned by people who liked to discipline. They were owned by moms like Bella's mom Wendy, who used Friday Tea to get her nails done.

The little girl pointed a finger as if it were a wand and declared, "She's going to be called Uni Uni."

"That's a good name, Bella." Maggie iced another cupcake. She felt eyes on her. She didn't look up, though. She'd been seeing Bella's grandma looking at her for a while. Then again, she knew Dotty was mesmerized with her eyes. Every time she came, Dotty's daughter would leave to have Mommy Alone Time and Dotty would help play tea party.

Maggie liked Dotty. She was very much a grandma, with white hair and soft makeup that clung to the fine hairs on her face.

"Everyone needs two cupcakes," Bella declared. "And don't forget Daddy's. He'll need two, too." She stopped and giggled. "Two, too. Tutu, tutu, tutu!"

Maggie smiled. She missed this age. It was a stubborn age, but it wasn't as…sullen as age eight could be. "Is your Daddy coming today?"

In the two years Maggie had been putting on Friday Teas, she had never seen anyone resembling a dad around here.

Dotty moved to stand next to her, and in a low voice she said, "Bella's Daddy sort of isn't full-time around here."

Maggie got the hint and didn't ask more questions about the MIA dad.

Something she knew just the teeniest, tiniest thing about.

Bella licked frosting off a cupcake, put it down, and then picked up another one to do the exact same thing: lick and discard. "Are you coming on Mommy's Day, too, Maggie?"

Maggie smiled as she iced more cupcakes. "No, I have my own little girl. I'll be with her."

"Oh." She licked off more pink icing. "But I like when you make the parties. Mommy doesn't make parties."

"On Mother's Day, *you* are the one making the party for *your* mommy. Do you know what you're going to do for her?"

Maggie pulled her sweater together and buttoned the first couple of buttons. The sun was out but the weather still held a chill. Beach days wouldn't come until June.

Bella must've felt the same cold breeze.

"I think Uni Uni needs a blanket!" And with that pronouncement, little Bella and her tutu and Uni Uni tucked into her tutu skipped to the house.

Maggie eyed her watch. Every Friday, Bella got a tea party from 10 until noon. There were only fifteen minutes left for today's party.

"You can leave if you need to. I won't tell her mother."

Maggie looked up to see the older woman smiling at her. "I can't leave when no one's had seconds." She shot Dotty a smile and refilled every human's and stuffed animal's cup. Except Bear Bear's. She dumped that in the grass.

"Gotta make her think Bear Bear is thirsty," Maggie explained.

"You're a class act, m'dear."

"Just living out the story."

"You're giving that little girl magic." Dotty picked up the cake in front of Bear Bear, took a small nibble, and placed it back on the plate. "Not enough people take the time to create magic anymore."

"I'm no David Copperfield."

Dotty waved the words away, like an unwelcome gnat. "David Copperfield has no magic in him. I'm talking about Santa flying around the world in one night kind of magic. Pumpkins transformed into coaches kind of magic."

"That's fairytale."

"It's recorded magic. Did it once exist? Who knows. But I think it did."

Dotty seemed a bit, well...dotty. Maggie knew it was coming from a good place, though, and so she didn't put up a fight. "I definitely don't have that sort of magic."

"You'd be surprised," Dotty said. A small smile twitched along her mouth.

"If I had magic, trust me," Maggie said as she adjusted Bear Bear so his paw was touching the cupcake, "I would be using it for myself this weekend."

Dotty ate a cupcake off of Cat Cat's plate. Her mouth still had cake in it as she said, "Tell me what's happening that makes you need to have magic this weekend."

What the hell. There were ten minutes left and no little ears around "I'm seeing my mom. *And* sisters. *And* nieces and nephews." Maggie listed everyone like they were the chores she thought they were.

"Don't like them too much, I take it?"

"Let's just say that if men are from Mars and women are from Venus, then they're from Florida and I'm…in a parallel dimension where the world is flipped upside down."

"Meaning?"

"Meaning that if I say 'What a pretty day! The sky is so blue.' Then one of them will say 'I think it's purple. Red, really."

Dotty chuckled and Maggie brought her the pitcher of lemonade. "Can I top you off, Dotty?"

"No, I better not. At my age, the bladder is not my friend."

Maggie closed her eyes and let herself feel the sun. Inside the house, Bella sang a song about a snowman. Maggie smiled. Roxie loved that damn song, too.

"You need a boy, don't you."

Maggie's eyes popped open. "Excuse me?"

"Sorry. I mean you need a 'man.' At my age, anyone under 50 is a boy."

Maggie tried to follow the conversation. She failed. "Dotty, can you treat me like I'm six? Because I'm not following you at all."

"That's okay. Sometimes I get a little ahead of the

client."

"Client?" Okay. Now Maggie really felt lost.

Dotty started to pry herself out of the Adirondack lawn chair she had settled into, but she didn't quite get the leverage she needed. She squirmed and got nowhere.

"Need a hand?" Maggie put her hand out, pressing her lips together to keep Dotty from seeing the smile wanting to come out.

The older woman put out a liver-spotted hand and Maggie pulled. "Aging sucks," Dotty said once she was up. "Try to avoid it if you can."

"I'll do my best."

A door slammed and Bella came out, stopping when she stepped down on the deck. She started tiptoeing over the deck, as if she was trying to avoid stepping on any cracks.

And there were a lot of cracks between those wood planks.

"I like you." Dotty nodded her head, as if she were agreeing with herself.

Maggie picked up a crumpled napkin that had fallen under the table. "You seem quite sure of that."

"I am. I like you and I'm going to help you." She put a card in Maggie's hand. It was a clear card, business-sized. Three letters were on it:

R A M
We make the magic happen.

"Ever hear of us?" Dotty asked.

Maggie stared at the card then back at the woman

who had handed it to her. She took in the bright red reading glasses that hung on a chain around her neck and the pearl earrings clipped to her thick, soft earlobes.

"Us?" Maggie finally asked. She wasn't sure what she was supposed to say or do. Truthfully, too many other things were on her mind.

Pack up everything here.

Unpack enough to find Roxie's headbands.

Confirm with the hotel that the suite was still booked.

Meet up with Roxie's bus after school.

Finish the gift bags.

Finish gathering materials for the games to be played at Jamison's party.

Figure out "Ian."

Run your ass off tonight.

"Me and my sister Dolly," the other woman was saying. "We're the Ram sisters."

That made something in Maggie's head ping. "I've think I've heard something?"

She tried to remember what it had been exactly, but she couldn't quite formulate a visual.

"We're in the rental business." Dotty said the words like she was divulging something.

And that's when Maggie realized who Dotty Ram was. The gray fog that had been clinging to a vague memory lifted.

She had definitely heard of Dorothy Ram and Dolores Ram. She giggled.

"You rent men!" Maggie heard her voice and it was loud. She fought to lower it. She also fought the shock and titillation she was feeling at knowing who this sweet-looking grandma was.

Dorothy Ram and Dolores Ram were *legends* along the New Hampshire seacoast.

"We do rent men, yes. But not in a Heidi Fleiss kind of way."

"Is there any other way?" Maggie posed. She wasn't being judgmental. She was honestly being curious.

"We provide men for those who need them. Sort of like providing food stamps to those who need food."

Maggie couldn't quite wrap her head around that definition. "So what you do is…welfare?"

Dotty twisted her mouth, thinking about Maggie's words. "Welfare is free to the person needing it. Our men, however, are not free. So maybe not food stamps. Maybe more like…providing bottled water to people on a hot summer day in the Sahara."

Dotty nodded, happy with her more apropos definition.

Bella's grandma rented men.

The thought was so, so…entertaining!

Maggie leaned forward, keeping her voice low. Bella was close to finishing the cracks on the deck. "So you're an honest to goodness madam?"

Dotty waved away her words. "No, but what a fun title *that* would be! A madam, however, creates a business where sexual favors are the expected product."

"And they…aren't?"

"No, they aren't." Dotty twisted her mouth and looked past Maggie, her hands on her hips in a defensive pose, as she said, "Now, if a couple decides to go this route themselves, that's up to them as two grown, consenting adults."

Dotty put on her red glasses and looked back at

Maggie. Looked her up and down. It gave Maggie a funny feeling in her stomach. "You need a man. So talk."

"I can't rent a guy, Dotty."

"Why?" she replied matter-of-factly.

"Because..it's nuts!" And probably expensive. She so couldn't do expensive.

What does that say about you, Magdalene Abigail Weston, to think about the money first? Think about how it's wrong *first!*

Dotty pulled out a notepad from a fanny pack at her waist. "So tell me. Tall, short, fat, thin?"

"Dotty!" Maggie laughed.

"What?"

"Are you serious?" She lowered her voice and looked behind her. Bella was still treating the deck's cracks like they were hot lava.

"Tall. Short. Fat. Thin." Dot said the words more slowly. And adamantly.

"Are you being serious here?"

"Of course. And trust me, I *can* help." Dotty raised a snow-white eyebrow. It appeared that she was one with her age, with no evidence of hair dyes, wrinkle creams, or medical interventions. "Now talk to me."

Maggie didn't say anything.

This was weird. Very, very weird.

"My dear." Dotty took on an air of Reassuring Grandma. "We don't have much time to find you someone, given that the weekend starts in, oh, twelve hours."

Dotty began to sit back down in the Adirondack, stopped herself, and made her way to the table set for

Bella's tea party. Maggie hurried ahead of her and picked up Bear Bear and the stack of books he'd been sitting on.

Dotty sat down. She took back Bear Bear and set him in her lap. "Okay then. Give me the basics of what you'd like to see in a man."

Maggie didn't know what to make of Dotty. She knew all about RAM Rentals because its reputation had preceded it. It was the odd and crazy little secret that everyone knew about and small-talked about with a smile.

Did Maggie want to be tied to a odd and crazy secret when she already had so much working against her?

"Dotty, I appreciate the offer but—"

"But nothing, honey. I'm pretty sure I have the perfect man for you, one who will look pretty on your arm and who will make your sisters die a little inside."

The mention of her sisters being jealous gave Maggie a moment to think. The idea of renting a man was…odd. Crazy.

But at the same time, it was interesting. And Maggie's life was nothing if not interesting. And if she rented a man with the express wish/want/guideline that there would be absolutely no sex…then maybe she could let herself do it?

As Dotty had so forcefully reminded her, Maggie had twelve hours before the weekend started. But she also had Jamison's party on Sunday.

Did she have time to find a guy who was okay with no strings *and* not being paid attention to all weekend?

"So." Dotty's pen hovered over the notebook. "Are you going to let me help?"

MAGGIE REALIZED that she had to let her gut decide. Her brain and her heart were too busy still arguing with each other.

And so her gut decided.

"I need a man for my mom. I mean, the man's for me, but what he'll be like should be stuff my mom likes." She paused and squinted into the bright blue sky overhead. This situation would be more palatable if she thought about it in terms of what Abigail Weston would like. "She likes tall. She hates when I wear heals and tower over a guy. She likes a guy to be financially independent, too, working because he wants to and not because he's paying a mortgage."

She had two fingers already out, and then she listed more things until all five fingers were out. "He must know how to dance, he must love 1960s sitcoms, and he must know every word to *The Sound of Music*."

Dot had a grin as she wrote down the laundry list of Maggie's wants. "You wanting this guy to be good in the sack?"

Maggie snorted. "No."

"No?"

"I live in a one-bedroom apartment with my eight-year-old. I have no room or privacy for a roll in the sack. This guy is strictly a beard for me."

Dotty stopped writing and pinned her gaze on Maggie. The look was intense. "My friend Charles has a beard. Me, when we go see his 90-year-old, very old-school Catholic grandmother in Martha's Vineyard." She put down her pen and leaned back. Some of the wind seemed to have been taken out of her sails. "Are you a lesbian? I don't care one way or the other, but I'm not going to waste good resources on something that has no hope of happening."

"Uh, no. Not in this lifetime, at least." Maggie sat next to Dolly, her pink and turquoise striped apron hammocked between her knees. "I wished that I sometimes was. It would make life so, so much easier. It would also double my shoe selection." Maggie scraped at a piece of dried icing on her hem. "But I can't exactly bring a guy to my pull-out couch while the kid's in the next room."

Dotty had perked up noticeably. The pen was back in her hand and a smile had found its way back onto her lips. "There's always his place."

Maggie gave Dotty's closest knee a light rap with the back of her fingers. "Hey now. I can't exactly put Rox on a leash and tie her outside, can I."

"'Fraid not." The woman with the salty reputation wrote down a few things. Maggie wondered if it was too late to get off this train. It was moving faster and faster, and pretty soon, she wouldn't be able to jump off.

Her gut told her to stay on.

Her brain and her heart, though, were not.

Chapter Six

AS DOTTY WROTE, SHE TALKED. "I remember raising my own kids. I had a husband. Herb. He never did much in the way of helping out lot, or if he did, it made more work for me."

Roxie's dad was more helpful being gone than being around. Maggie had known that when they first met, but she had ignored the signs because he was supposed to be a fun fling.

But then she got pregnant.

And now her fling was a permanent fixture.

"But he was around?" Maggie asked.

"More or less. Knowing he was around made it easier." Dot looked up. "You must be getting pretty tired of going it alone, huh?"

Maggie was more than tired. But that wasn't what was on her mind right now.

"How much is it going to cost me?" Maggie had money in the bank for food. Money for the clothes

Roxie seemed to be outgrowing every other week. Money for the membership to the $20-a-month gym across the street that had working treadmills she could take her stress out on.

She didn't have disposable income for a babysitter. Or clothes that were full price. Or chicken that was free range, organically fed, and sung to sleep by Bavarian monks.

But maybe, just maybe, she could use some of that dwindling nest egg to rent a guy for one weekend.

And to show her mom and her sisters that she wasn't a Bad Mom.

The sun was high, almost noon if not already noon. She soaked in the light, briefly closing her eyes and listening to the scratch of Dotty writing as Bella continued to sing about that damn snowman.

"It will cost you more than a bread box but less than the Hope Diamond," Dotty said.

"That doesn't help me much."

The older woman looked up. "This guy doesn't need to be good in the sack?"

"No."

"Is this a guy who *wants* to be naked with a woman?"

"I want a guy who can sing *The Sound of Music*, Dotty. I'm not expecting anyone who thinks about boobs or what he could do with them."

The older lady kept writing and didn't answer her.

The figure must be a lot.

Okay. Now she was nervous. Maggie pulled out her phone and scrolled through her phone contacts, looking for someone who could pull off being a part-time fiancé and would expect absolutely nothing in return.

sydney*strand*

Maybe a gay guy friend?

She had three. Paul, who lived too far away in London. Charles, who was on a babymoon with his hubby before their surrogate gave birth next month. But the third one…

"You know what? I'm sure I have someone I can call who will help me out," Maggie said.

"Someone who's willing to turn and walk away when you're done with him Sunday night?"

Maggie scrolled down. "Sure."

"Is this man going to stay with you at the hotel?"

"Yes."

"In the same suite?"

"If I can get my gay guy friend to do it, sure. But anyone who is even the teeniest bit hetero? Uh, no. My daughter will be with me."

She thought about her Roxie. Smurf-obsessed, compassionate, sometimes-mouthy Roxie Riveter Weston. Roxie, who was the cat's pajamas and the kitty's meow.

She'd do whatever she had to for that kid. Even if that meant Mommy Doesn't Get a Boyfriend to Have Sex With Until Her Baby Goes Off to College.

Maggie found the number. She dialed, and Royce picked up on the second ring.

He answered with, "Babe! I got your message. Totally sad to see you bail."

Maggie thought about the cabin and the distant memory of how this weekend *should have* been playing out. "I'm not bailing. I'm being responsible."

"I had it totally blinged out for you, too. Even installed a disco ball."

Maggie groaned. She loved to dance with Roxie. Adored it, as a matter of fact. "Shut up."

"Would if I could but I can't," Royce gloated.

Maggie smiled. Royce would a good guy. He'd rented to her in Oceanview, and while he hadn't been able to do basic things like fix a running faucet or a clogged disposal, he had been masterful at sewing. Her drapes, her duvet cover, and one really slutty Little Black Dress were thanks to Royce.

"I'm calling you for a reason." She explained the weekend ahead of her. "And I need a guy who's safe."

"Thanks for making me feel like a eunuch, dearie."

"Oh, I'm sure you're a beast with the men, if that helps any."

"Slightly." Someone said something on Royce's end. "I'd love to help you, love, but my own mother is in town. Who is nothing like your mother. She's utterly fantastic."

In the background, Maggie heard, "It's easy when I have a fantastic son."

Ignoring the disappointment twisting her stomach, Maggie said her goodbyes and hung up. She scrolled through her list of contacts one more time before flipping off her phone.

Every hetero guy in there was either related to her, thousands of miles away building wells or fighting wars, or would expect something at the end of the weekend. Maggie had no time or energy for that kind of guy.

Which meant one thing: she would have to rent a man. A guy who wouldn't expected anything out of her. No kisses, no sex, no explanations for why she didn't call.

"You want me to rent you someone, Maggie?" Dotty shaded her eyes with a hand and glanced toward the house. Bella was almost to them, no shoes on, Uni Uni tucked under the sash of her dress. Soap from the bathroom's foam soap dispenser covered an elbow and her nose.

It looked like she was going to have to clean up Bella.

Then she was going to have to clean up the tea party.

And then she was going to have to rent a man.

 *Chapter Seven*

"HEY, HEAD'S UP. I've got a client who needs a man."

Dolly Ram put a towel behind one knee and pulled it toward her. It was old lady yoga, but it helped her arthritis.

But to her, age was a number. She was sixty-five, but she felt thirty-five, all thanks to old lady yoga. And maybe just the tiniest bit of herbs and oils and the right words said under the right moon.

"Who needs a man?" Dolly asked.

"Maggie Weston."

"Maggie with the big blue eye and the big green eye and the red hair and that smile?" Dolly pulled her knee closer, blowing out as she did. "The one you talk about every Friday afternoon? From what you've told me, she's a pretty little thing. She can get someone all by herself."

"She needs a man by tomorrow."

"She's in Oceanview, right?"

"Maple Woods. She just moved."

Dolly extended her knee and blew out. "Then have her sit at a table over at the The Coffee Pot. She'll attract a handful of suitors before dinner."

"She doesn't want a relationship."

"It doesn't have to be a relationship."

"The way that lady looks," Dotty said, walking further into Dolly's office, "trust me, she has a way of making guys want a relationship with her. To put babies into her. To tie her up and never let her go."

Dolly scowled from where she was crunching up to meet her knee. "Dotty, sometimes your mind scares me." Breathe in, breathe out. "I'm perfectly okay if you don't share *everything* with me."

"It's the truth." Dotty held up a check. Bright red pen was scrawled across it. "Anyway, it's a done deal. I just wanted to give you a head's up."

"She already paid?" Dolly stopped mid-crunch. Around here, people liked paying in pumpkin butter and apple cider donuts.

"Yes. So give her your best." Dotty sat down on the sofa covered in a flower print and amongst needlepointed pillows of Me and Ow, Dolly's Siamese cats. Me and Ow were sisters from the same litter. Just like Dolly and Dotty, who had been born five minutes apart.

But Me and Ow were a heck of a lot less catty to one another.

They only time the sisters got along were the four days of the year when one season changed into the next. Those were the days when the wind shifted and the earth just felt different.

Dolly sat up, popping the gum she always seemed to have in her mouth. "She needs no strings?"

"Exactly."

"And she knows this weekend is Mother's Day weekend? That it might scare off a lot of guys we'd otherwise have access to?"

Dotty nodded. "She knows very well it's Mother's Day weekend. That's part of the reason she needs a man."

"Meaning…"

"Meaning we need a guy who doesn't have a mom around to visit and who doesn't mind going out with moms. We need someone with a great sense of who he is and where he's going. Someone who's not going to make a big deal out of being with a mom on 'her' day."

Dolly pulled up her leg and pulsed it. "She knows what we do?"

"She knows enough." Dotty watched her sister's leg. "Be careful there, Wonder Woman. We wouldn't want you pulling something."

"Shut up, old lady."

"Right back at ya." Dotty gave an exaggerated grimace in Dolly's direction as she pried herself off the sofa and went to Dolly's desk. The key was in the right bottom drawer's lock, so opening it was easy enough. Dolly went nowhere without that key, the only copy.

Dotty pulled her eyes off the elusive key and dug out a black three-ring binder marked **Q-S**.

Dolly's lips thinned. She didn't like people in her drawer.

"Who are you lookin' for, sister dear?" Dolly asked.

"I'm thinking New Hampshire University men." She

flipped pages. "Professors. Deans."

"You have Q through S in your hands there. You must be thinking of someone."

Dotty ignored her as she flipped to a page she seemed to be looking for.

Dolly knew which page that was.

The page with *him* on it.

"You can't have Augustus," Dolly ordered.

"No one owns him." Dotty pulled a little notebook from her fanny pack and jotted something down.

Augustus Sloane was a catch. A *big* catch. The equivalent of Moby Dick. He was six-foot-two, crazy smart, and smelled like the outdoors. It didn't hurt that he had muscles that made a woman weak just knowing he could pick you up, even if you were carrying a few extra pounds.

Dotty couldn't have him. "You can't have him," Dolly warned.

"Luckily, *I* don't want him."

"You know what I mean. That Melissa of yours can't have him."

"Maggie."

"Whatever. I have plans for him."

"You can't call dibs on a human being."

"For that human being I can." She scowled. "Give her someone else."

"But no one else owes us anything huge at the moment, and this is a huge favor we're asking. Anyway, what's the deal? Why can't she have Augustus?" Dotty challenged. "Did you already book him?"

Dolly gently dabbed under her nose with the corner of her hand towel. "The plans aren't in place yet," Dolly hedged. "Alyssa hasn't come to me yet."

"Well, Maggie *did* come to me, like I knew she would." Dotty grabbed the page featuring Augustus Sloane, Ph.D., M.D., and pulled. "He's my Maggie's now."

That got Dolly to roll up until she was sitting on her butt. Dolly didn't believe in computer back-ups or even computers in general. This piece of paper was the one and only copy she had with Dr. Augustus Sloane's stats and the dirt she had on him.

Getting from her butt to her feet was going to be a five-minute endeavor, though, with the creaky knees yoga had helped but hadn't cured. "Put him back!"

"Nope."

"Augustus owes me, not you," Dolly huffed. She was now on her hands and knees, steeling herself to the next-to-worst part: heaving herself up onto one knee.

"He doesn't know who did what. He just knows one of us did it, and I plan to cash in on that right now."

Dolly struggled to get off the one knee that still kept her on the floor. Her face was hot and her hair was more in her face than in its ponytail. "You're a real butthole sometimes, Dotty."

Her sister didn't hear her.

She was already gone, off to steal the company's best product.

Chapter Eight

"DR. SLOANE?"

The sophomore hung outside the lab door, afraid to disturb the hulking man bent over a microscope and taking notes without looking at what he was writing. After a semester in his class, she knew Augustus Sloane, Ph.D., M.D., well enough to keep a healthy distance from him when he was working on a problem.

Of course, she'd one day like to keep a *less* healthy distance. The tall strawberry blonde had biceps that didn't belong on a scientist. They were tan and strained at the ribbed edge of his short-sleeved polo shirt. Boy did they strain.

She jumped when he barked, "Talk!"

"I..." Most of the students at NHU were quivering messes around this guy. She might've looked like she took no shit with her piercings and her purple hair, but she still had nerves. And feelings. And right now, she felt really, really intimidated.

She swallowed, and her gum went down with her saliva. She didn't try to talk until after she stopped coughing. "I was hoping you could talk to me about the final?"

He adjusted the focus of the microscope and kept his head down. "Did you read the book?"

"Yes."

"Did you take notes?"

"I highlighted."

"Take notes." He didn't say more than that, and the girl knew she had been dismissed. She turned to go and almost collided with a white haired woman wearing a cat sweatshirt and a turquoise fanny pack.

The heat in the girl's cheeks got worse. "Sorry! I didn't see you there."

She didn't say much more because Augustus was still talking. "If you're going to pass this final, Miss Adams, you better get yourself home to start writing out those notes."

"Yes Dr. Sloane!" A chipmunk on helium. That's what she sounded like.

She rushed past the old woman, tripping over her feet as she headed to the doors that would take her back in the direction of her dorm.

Her cheeks hurt. She raised a hand and felt the smile on her mouth.

Dr. Sloane had known her name. Three hundred students were in Entomology 101 and he knew *her* name.

Suddenly, taking notes as she re-read four-hundred pages about bugs over the next three days didn't seem so horribly painful.

Chapter Nine

ONCE THE DOOR WAS CLOSED, Dotty stopped biting her tongue. "You better watch out, Augustus. That young baby of a girl doesn't know your bark is worse than your bite."

"That's not quite true. My bite can leave some marks." Augustus looked up from his microscope just enough to give her a smile. "Polka Dot?"

The girl who'd just tripped out of here wasn't the only one affected by a certain Augustus Sloane. Dotty blushed. "The one and only. You can always figure out Dolly. She's got the scar through her right eyebrow."

"Knife fight?"

"Raggedy Andy fight back when we were three. Our mother should've gotten us two of 'em. She learned soon enough that I punched first and asked questions later."

Augustus snorted out a laugh in the large lab fitted with long tables, Bunsen burners, and hundreds of microscopes bolted to the countertops.

Dotty found herself thinking a snort had never sounded so sexy.

She just stood there and took in 38-year-old Augustus Sloane, Ph.D., M.D. Augustus had taken a page from Dotty's playbook and didn't put much time into his looks, letting the silver strands of gray stay where they were amongst the strawberry blonde of his hair. The lines at his eyes were caused by spending hours outside studying the world. The nails on his hands were bluntly cut by clippers wielded by a hurried hand.

He was a fine specimen of a male. Her sister and her sister's potential client didn't need Augustus Sloane, Ph.D., M.D.

Her Maggie Weston did, though. Especially if she was going to see how much better life could be if she didn't have to go it alone, acting like she had to be better than the average mom because she *was* alone.

Maggie didn't have to be alone.

Not with a man like Augustus Sloane, Ph.D., M.D., in the world.

"DOTTY. TALK OR GO." Augustus reluctantly pulled his eyes away from the slide of pulverized mosquito. He rubbed his eyes, willing them to be less dry and to focus again. He had the bad feeling he was the closest he'd ever been to getting glasses. A real pisser considering he was always outside, and glasses would slow him down.

He'd have to get regular glasses and prescription

sunglasses, and he'd have to keep changing them out.

Or he could just wear a pair around his neck like Dotty. He didn't care what people thought about him, so that could be a real hoot.

Maybe even get bright red ones just like Polka Dot's.

"First of all, you can keep a nice tone of voice when you're talking to me," she lectured.

He stole a quick glance at her. "Sorry Polka Dot. I forget my manners when I've got deadlines."

"We've all got deadlines, hon. But we all don't have to face that tone of voice. Work on it, huh?"

The professor already knew this. He would be a lot higher up on the career ladder if he hadn't pissed off the wrong people over the years. He was blunt, very blunt. If someone was fat, he told them. If someone was being dumb, he told them. He wasn't on this earth to exchange pleasantries. He was here to make a difference.

And right now, that meant making humans resistant to mosquito-born illnesses. It was possible. He was *thisclose* to making it possible.

"I apologize Polka Dot. "

Dotty brushed at a lab table with her hand. The cleaning crew had wiped everything down last night, and the lab hadn't been used since then, so Augustus knew she was biding time. Sure enough, it took her only a little bit longer to get out her next words: "I've got a favor to ask."

"Yeah?" He pulled away from the microscope and leaned his long body against the stainless steel lab table. He crossed his legs at the ankle, wincing when he tweaked the shin splint that had been growing all week.

He had time for his five-mile jogs each morning, but he didn't have time to do the maintenance stuff, like go to an eye doc or ice his leg or go to university get-togethers where you had to talk about nothing and laugh at nothing.

Instead, his time and energy was being sucked up by one of the biggest challenges of his life. The great state of New Hampshire had a big, fat problem when it came to mosquitos. The fellow currently under his microscope was from the *Culex pupiens* species. They were nasty little suckers who spread West Nile and Eastern Equine Encephalitis like the, well, plagues they were.

If his research played out like he hoped, Augustus could help curtail how easily one of those suckers could infect a human with a debilitating or deadly disease.

Dotty was talking again, but he'd missed what she'd said.

He reluctantly tuned back in. "Can you repeat that again, Polka Dot?"

She sighed and rolled her eyes. "Really, Augustus, what I have to say is time sensitive information. Listen up! What I was saying is that I want to set you up with a lovely woman by the name of—"

"No." He went back to the microscope.

"You didn't let me finish, Augustus," she chastised.

He didn't look up. "I know where it's going. I just finished the thought for you."

"You do know that while you *are* brilliant, you are *not* clairvoyant. Unless you are. Tell me now if you are because I'll shut up knowing that you truly knew what I was going to say and will say. I can save my breath then.

A woman my age needs her breath."

He closed his eyes and sighed. His *thisclose* breakthrough would have to wait. "Fine, Dot. Tell me what I don't know."

"That's Aunt Dot to you."

"Yes, Aunt Dot."

She crossed her arms over her screen-printed tabby and gave him the stink eye. All Ram women had a gift with stink eye, and his own mother had been especially great at it.

Being around his aunts made Augustus feel that his mother was still alive, giving guff and taking no prisoners. It could sometimes annoy him, but he mostly loved it.

"I have a girl who needs a no-strings fellow this weekend. This weekend only, by the way."

"You want to set me up with this woman?"

"Yes."

He took in a breath and blew it out. He knew what his aunts did, and he didn't want to get sucked into it. "No."

He turned back to his microscope.

"This girl is gorgeous."

"Good for her."

"She can get any man she wants."

"Great. Let her get one."

"She wants one with no strings, Augustus."

"So get her one with no strings."

"Augustus Regis Sloane! You look at me right now!"

He took his eyes off *Culex pupiens* and focused on his new source of trouble. He was under deadline to get his findings to Bethesda, home to Health and Human

Services. It wasn't an insane deadline, but it was a deadline nonetheless.

Because this wasn't just about mosquitoes and the lives they affected. It was also about his life and where it needed to head.

And New Hampshire University was no longer the finish line.

"This *girl*." He finally engaged with his aunt. His students thought he could be surly, but he didn't hold a candle to Dorothy Ram when she was upset. Her husband died ten years ago, and now she had no patience for disagreements that weren't going her way. "Exactly how old is she?"

Anyone under thirty would feel like it was one of his students. This conversation was dead in the water if—

"She's thirty-four. Has a kid, too."

"That's not the way to persuade me to go out with her, Polka Dot," he said.

She held up a finger. "What did I say about tone, buddy? Watch it." The stink eye glared at him. "I'm not talking about anything permanent here. She needs a guy for this weekend and that's it."

Augustus was done with this conversation. He was done and just wanted to get back to the liquified mosquito. "Why this weekend exactly? Does she need a wedding date?" God, he loathed weddings.

"No, she doesn't need a wedding date." She seemed to wince before she got her next set of words out. "She needs someone to meet her mom. To pretend that you two are engaged."

This was like shooting fish in a barrel. "No."

He'd been willing to hear Dotty out, against his better

judgment. Going to a wedding had been a maybe. But meeting someone's mother was a definite *No*.

"Did I mention that if you do this for me, we'll be even?"

That got his attention. He pushed away from his microscope and stood up. "In full?"

She sighed and reluctantly confirmed he had heard correctly. "Yes. In full."

"How many days am I on the hook?"

"Two. Starting at 7 a.m. tomorrow. Ending at midnight Sunday. Well, I guess that would make it Monday."

Two long days with a thirty-four-year-old mom and her kid.

And her mom.

He tapped his palms against the black granite counter, thinking. He'd dated moms before. At his age, it was unavoidable. There were two that he had even dated for longer than a few months: the one with a sullen thirteen-year-old boy who looked like he wanted to deck Augustus whenever he saw him, and the six-year-old twins who had dressed in pink bows and white shoes and screamed whenever he pointed out a bug to them.

He was fine with moms. Their kids, though, were never fine with him.

And he had no idea what a date's mom would be like. He'd never met one of those before. He'd made sure of that.

But he had a debt to repay. A big one that had been hovering over his head for the last twenty years.

"Two days?" he asked.

"Yes."

"No strings?" he clarified.

"Yes."

He rubbed at his left bicep, massaging at the knot that was still there after last night's kayak on the Oyster River.

His life was divided between research, his teaching duties, and staying physically active. Ironically, he was the fittest he had ever been in his life, but his thirty-eight-year-old body was finding it harder to recover from the residual aches and pains.

Damn aging anyway.

But his body could definitely be worse off. That led him to his next thought:

Damn debts.

It was time to embrace the inevitable. "Make sure she isn't late, Dot, or I'm out of there."

Dotty gave him a big grin that showed off her shiny dentures. "I wouldn't be surprised if… No, I won't say it. I don't want to jinx it."

He rolled his eyes but let her have her hopes. After two days, his debt would be paid and it would be back to life as usual. Female-free and focused on the next rung on the ladder.

"Just bone up on your *Bewitched* before you meet this girl."

"*Bewitched*?"

"Please tell me you've heard of *Bewitched*!"

"It was that witch show from the 1960s, right?"

"Yeah, that's the one." Dotty pulled out the notebook she had written her notes in. "And see if you can learn the words to 'Do Re Mi' while you're at it."

 *Chapter Ten*

"MAGGIE! YOO HOO! MAGGIE!"

Maggie looked up from where she had just inserted her keys into the Jeep Cherokee's lock. Dotty Ram was waving her down as she walked down the sidewalk, favoring her left hip, one hand on her fanny pack, the other on her lower back.

Maggie was stunned to see her. This was Maggie's town. That meant she couldn't have Dotty around in *her* town. Not unless she wanted to be known as not just the Bad Mom, but the Bad Mom Who Rents a Man.

"Dotty. Hey! This is Jessa. I don't think you know her, since you live in Oceanview and she lives here in town." She gestured to the woman standing next to her, a tall brunette holding a clipboard containing a to-do checklist and colored print-outs of Pinterest photos. "Jessa owns The Store Basket."

Dotty's eyes grew wide. "Oh, honey, I go out of my way each week to pick up your pumpkin whoopie pies.

Do you make those?"

"My head baker does, yes." Jessa was eyeing the older woman with a mixture of politeness and tension. Dotty was keeping them from an appointment that had them getting a tour of the town's one and only hotel and its presidential suite.

Maggie was so screwed if Jessa hated the room. She was willing to bet Roxie's entire Smurf collection that Jessa had a tape measure in her purse to measure the room, log the numbers, and figure out the square footage for each girl.

Speaking of Roxie…a quick look at her watch showed that Roxie's bus came in thirty more minutes.

"Can we talk a little later, Dotty?" Maggie opened her door and Jessa walked to the Range Rover parked in front of her. It was a gorgeous car, with a pristine fender: no dents, no scratches, no 10 years' worth of bumper stickers with three guys who had never become president. "The bus will be here soon and I need to meet it."

The older woman came closer, her white leather Keds squeaking as she walked, and she dropped her voice. "I found someone."

"Great. Fantastic." Maggie stole a quick look at the Range Rover. Jessa had started it and was fiddling with the air controls.

"He'll meet you in front of The Coffee Pot tomorrow at seven a.m. Sharp. He's got a thing for punctuality."

"That's a thing I'm okay with." Maggie's stomach churned a bit. But she ignored it. Her brain was trying to tell her this was a piss poor idea. Well, her brain wasn't the one making decisions here.

Her gut was still in charge.

"He's a scientist." Dotty wasn't going anywhere, even when Maggie slid in and started the engine. "He teaches at the college. Tenured, too. He also does work for the the government."

"Two jobs, huh?" So much for finding a man that didn't need to work.

Dotty gave a wink that made her seem like a young woman of maybe fifty. "He doesn't *need* to work, though. He made a couple of inventions in his teens that have set him up quite well."

Scientist? Inventions? Maggie let herself finally breathe for the first time since she'd told her mom "Ian" would be coming.

This scientist guy had no-strings written all over him. Out of every kind of man out there, nothing did less for her than some overly cerebral guy who thought he was the smartest guy in the room.

"What does he look like?" She told herself she was asking for her mom. She didn't care.

She told herself.

"Like Redford. But bigger. Strappier."

A ginger. Not something that turned her on, but her mom had always had a thing for Prince Harry. So that was a go. "And 60s sitcoms and *The Sound of Music*? Dancing?"

"That's stuff you'll need to ask him, sweet pea. You guys need something to talk about, right?"

Maggie heard Jessa shift the car and, sure enough, the taillights came on. She was in reverse and waiting on Maggie to move her ass.

Maggie knew she had to wrap this up, but she was

still compelled to blurt out, "It feels weird buying a man, Dotty."

"You're not buying him, honey, you're renting him. For two days. Augustus is good with that."

"Augustus?" That name was a definite mood killer. And another chalk mark in the column of "No Strings Attached!"

"His father was a scholar of the Roman Empire," Dotty was saying.

Maggie could see an academic nerd naming his son a nerd name. "Well, thanks. I appreciate you doing this for me."

"Trust me, you're doing *me* a favor."

"How exactly?" Movement caught Maggie's eye. Was that the English dude she had met at The Coffee Pot? He he had traded his gray fleece and jeans for a white button-down and khakis.

And he was leading a small battalion of kids down the sidewalk, like a duck with the entire flock's ducklings.

Dotty broke into her thoughts: "Do you know Noah Fisher?"

That's right. That was his name. "We met briefly this morning. I know nothing about him, just his name."

"He teaches at Abenaki Elementary. Third grade, I believe. Your daughter goes there, doesn't she?"

"She does. She's a second grader." She was watching Noah Fisher more closely now. He was laughing with two of the kids at the front of the line, his sleeves rolled up to his elbows, his aviators still on. And for the first time, she noticed the long lines dimpling his cheeks.

"Earth to Maggie."

She snapped her eyes back to Dotty. She tuned in and

heard her say, "Don't forget. Seven tomorrow, at The Coffee Pot." The older woman grinned. "You're going to love him."

And she left as abruptly as she had come.

Tomorrow, Maggie was going to meet a big, huge nerd. A nerd that had cost her five hundred dollars. Money she didn't really have. Money that had come out of her emergency fund.

He better be worth every single shiny red cent.

Because right now, she needed a man that money had bought. *A man with no strings.*

And as she told herself that, her eyes followed Noah Fisher, third grade teacher.

Chapter Eleven

"YOU AWAKE, LITTLE ME?"

Maggie kept her voice low and soft, in case her eight-year-old had dropped off in the five minutes since she had finished brushing her teeth.

"Yep." Roxie turned her head, the light from the hall highlighting her sweet round cheeks and the honey hair falling across her pillow. Maggie walked to her, a glass of water in her hand.

"Thirsty?"

"Yes please."

Maggie came to the small body of her daughter, made smaller by the queen-sized bed that used to be Maggie's, and sat next to her. Roxie sat up and gulped the cool sink water. As she did, Maggie smoothed hair from her daughter's flushed cheek.

Maggie sat and enjoyed her child, even as the rolling ticker tape in her mind kept spitting out things to do.

E-mail Jessa!

Clean up the kitchen!
Unpack boxes!
Work out!

She couldn't go to the gym, not with Roxie in bed and it almost midnight, and she couldn't do anything that would pound her feet on the floor. Her downstairs neighbors wouldn't appreciate that too much.

That meant thirty minutes of Pilates. God, she hated that shit. It didn't help lower her stress at all.

"I had something I wanted to talk to you about," Maggie said slowly.

Roxie sat, listening.

Maggie took a breath, taking care in what she needed to say. "It's about a boy."

Roxie made a face. "Is it that George kid?"

George? Maggie took the empty water glass from Roxie, combing through her memory banks and all of her Roxie Conversations. "George in your class George? The kid who said he wanted to marry you?"

"Yeah."

"No, this isn't about George." He would definitely be no strings, though. He was eight and liked eating his fingernails. "You know how I said we were going somewhere real nice this weekend for Mother's Day?"

"Mr. Royce's cabin."

"Yes, Mr. Royce's cabin." She hoped Royce was having fun with his mom. Oceanview was great for a single gay man, chockfull of restaurants and clubs. But the school system had shown just too many failings, making Maggie quit and leave her two-bedroom apartment on Royce's "gentleman's" farm where Roxie had spent her afternoons feeding alpacas grass and chickens their seed. "But there's been a change in plans."

"We won't be going to the cabin?"

Maggie heard the disappointment in Roxie's voice. It made her sick to her stomach.

"What about the s'mores?" Roxie asked. "And diving for pirate treasure?"

"We're still going to do all that." The Montgomery had fire pits and a pool to throw gold-painted plastic eggs into the deep end, weighed down with rocks and a few quarters. A Maggie-and-Roxie tradition whenever they were near water. "But Grand wants us to get together as a family at The Montgomery."

"Grand is here?" That got Roxie to sit up, no sign of sleepiness now.

"Yes."

"And COUSINS?"

"Yep." Maggie knew that cousins would be the selling point here. She should've led with that.

Not a boy.

Boy, it sucked being tired all the time.

Roxie threw her arms around Maggie and Maggie pulled her close, breathing in the strawberry shampoo smell of her hair and feeling the soft fuzziness of her blue fleece pajamas, a faded, pilling Smurfette on the top. "Oh yay, Mommy, yay!"

Maggie held her and let the rolling ticker tape in her head keep rolling along.

Whether she started on the list now or thirty minutes from now didn't matter.

It would be late and she would be tired either way.

But thirty minutes from now, this moment would officially be a memory. Forever.

 *Chapter Twelve*

MAGGIE SHOVED HER HANDS deeper under her arms, trying to be even a tiny bit warm in the Kelly green cardigan she'd thrown over her black workout shirt and pants. She rocked back on her heels, studying the way her big toes were starting to wear through the top of her sneakers.

Oh yay. Yet another expense to add to the list.

She scanned the street, which was quiet for a Saturday morning. It was finals all week next week, and students were either sleeping in or studying.

Or they were just passed out drunk trying to forget about the week ahead.

The sun popped up at the top of the road, super bright but not hot enough to obliterate the cold morning. One person sat outside enjoying the day, his yellow Lab lying faithfully beside him. The dog kept looking at the guy's cream cheese Danish like it was the only thing that existed in his world.

Maggie envied that dog's life. So simple and easy.

She slipped on her sunglasses, cold and nervous and trying not to be.

This was a stupid, stupid idea.

"Are you the woman who needs the date?"

Maggie turned and saw a man who wore a scowl comfortably and a pair of loose nylon running shorts just as well. His thickly muscled quads and calves were on full display, and on a man who wasn't scowling, they would have been damn sexy.

Instead, they were pleasant on the man who, apparently, was not so pleasant.

"I'm the woman," Maggie concurred. She wasn't going to argue over a fact, even if it was rudely stated. "You're the man I've…booked?"

"I'm the man." He glanced at his watch, a chunky black plastic thing that probably took his heart rate and oxygen levels and worked as a Bluetooth device, too. An expensive-looking thing. "I came by five minutes ago. You weren't out yet."

Maggie looked at her cellphone. "Five minutes ago was 6:59."

"Exactly. You need to come early so that you can be on time."

Maggie was beginning to get a feel for this guy. She had a feeling this act made his students piss their pants.

Maggie, however, was just plain pissed.

"That's the dumbest thing I've ever heard. I was on time. Not *early* so I *could be* on time." She shook her head. Then her arms. Then her hands. Trying to get back to feeling good and optimistic. "Yes. I'm your date."

The dog that Maggie had been envying bumped into

the Scientist Jerk's leg. He scratched the dog under the chin, and the dog's tail whipped against the table leg so hard and fast, Maggie wondered if a tail could break.

What the hell was this guy's name again? Maximus? Atticus?

"When do you need me to start?" he asked.

"Nine this morning works."

"Through the weekend?" he continued.

"Yes."

"And the sleeping arrangements?"

"Separate rooms."

"Because of the kid?"

She snorted. "And because I don't know you."

"Let's remedy that then." He put out his hand. "Augustus Sloane."

Maggie shook it. There was no reason not to. "Maggie Weston." She kept a hold of his hand, and he raised an eyebrow when she did, but he didn't pull it away. "I don't know how much Dotty told you, but there's a weird catch to this."

"You mean pretending to be your fiancé while meeting your mother?" His eyes narrowed, and she could see the judgment. She didn't blame him. She was judging herself, too. "Yes. She told me."

"Did she tell you his name is Ian?"

"His name is—?" His eyes narrowed even more. "No. No she did not."

MAGGIE WESTON HAD DEFINITELY NOT been what he had been expecting.

Augustus made his way back to his house in the faculty neighborhood he'd moved into ten years ago. It was off Main Street, the next street over from The Coffee Pot.

He had been envisioning a mom like the moms he saw in this town. With a ponytail and mom jeans and a shirt with "Abenaki Elementary Soccer Club" across her chest.

He hadn't been envisioning a fellow redhead with tight black clothes showing a well-proportioned hip-to-waist-to-chest ratio and a smile that was almost unnaturally wide. Like a surgeon had slit the corners of her mouths just a tiny bit more than nature had intended.

Not in a Joker kind of way. It wasn't freaky, just…big. It reminded him of that one actress's mouth that he didn't enjoy watching. Nothing against the woman as a person, but he wasn't into glorifying hookers who got fairytale endings.

The wide smile was an unexpected phenomenon from an unexpected woman.

Who had asked him to answer to Ian.

That was a new one. Women had called him August. And Auggie. And one unfortunate soul attempted Gus when her hand was in his pants.

She might as well have dumped ice on him.

But he had a debt to repay. So he'd let this woman call him Ian. Even Gus, as long as she didn't have her hand in his pants. Which wasn't happening, according to Maggie and Dotty.

He turned and walked up the moss and stone path to his purple front door, a leftover from the previous tenant, an art professor. She was now in Manhattan, overseeing set decorations for Broadway musicals. She'd followed her dream and had actually gotten the damn thing.

And in weeks, maybe days, it would be his turn.

After fighting with the uncooperative 100-year-old lock, Augustus let himself into the three-bedroom cottage, his foot automatically squeaking the old pine floors. The wood-burning stove was still putting out heat, and he completely closed the damper to extinguish anything that was still burning inside.

He wouldn't be here again until late Sunday night. While he was gone, this street would come alive with barbecues and street hockey and scooter racing. Maybe even a lemonade stand would be attempted.

It was a street filled with cute trees, cute kids, and The American Dream.

But Augustus had seen the world, and he wanted to get back out there and see more of it. He had dreams, and they didn't include cute trees, cute kids, or potato salad that had been left in the sun for six hours.

He dropped his keys in the pink jewelry box by the front door and headed to his bedroom, where his clothes, duffel bag, and laptop were.

And he got ready to be Ian.

Chapter Thirteen

"SO WHO ARE YOU AGAIN?"

Roxie, The Eight Year Old to End All Eight Year Olds, sat in back of the Jeep Cherokee with red pigtails and a thing for blue. Even her chin rested on top of some fuzzy blue stuffed animal she had in a death grip on.

Augustus thought the girl was a little old to be dragging a toy around, but her mother didn't appear to mind.

It was a small strike against her. Maggie, not the girl.

He kept his eyes on the road, the steering wheel jerking under his hands. The Jeep needed to be serviced. Soon. "Ask your mother who I am."

"He's a friend of mine," Maggie supplied. She offered the information with a too-big smile and a distraction. "Do you want some Gummies, LaLa? They're in a most lovely Smurf shape."

Augustus crunched the stick shift to a lower gear, hoping to make the car think about going faster. But it was straining under their combined weight of two adults, a kid, and air.

If the care of this car was any indication about how Maggie was as a person, he wasn't feeling too good about how this weekend was going to play out.

"Mom's never talked about you." Roxie was still on the trail, ignoring her mother's pat answer.

Augustus tried to ignore the car and focus on the small human with an unnatural attachment to what appeared to be a blue troll. A Smurf, maybe? "Your mother's never talked about you, either, so we're even." He went back up to fifth gear. The gauge plummeted from 50 to 40. He downshifted back to fourth.

"What Mr. Sloane means to say, LaLa," Maggie said, an edge to her words that Augustus knew was meant for him, "is that I've been keeping you and our life private until I knew where our…relationship…was going."

"But we just moved to town. When did you guys start dating?"

The kid had her there.

Maggie, however, had her answer ready. "We used to live just half an hour away. Mr. Sloane has a car. I have a car. There are roadways that connect our two towns."

She hadn't actually lied to the kid. She hadn't actually put into words, "And we then went on dates."

His opinion of Maggie Weston went up a smidge.

There was silence from the back. Then: "You always said you'd never introduce me to a guy unless it was serious. Are you serious?"

The kid had her there.

"Think of Mr. Sloane as a friend. And I'd introduce you to a friend, right?"

Yet again, Maggie had successfully slid past the truth.

"Right." Roxie got silent, but Augustus swore he could hear the pieces of a puzzle being tested and shifted and snapped together in the back. "So why didn't you introduce him to me sooner if he's just a friend?"

The kid was a pip. Augustus gave a quick look in his left side mirror as he hid a quick smile.

Maggie kept her cool, he had to give her that. "I'm done answering questions for now, Rox. We'll pick the conversation back up when we go home, okay?"

The car took the ramp into Portsmouth, a seaside town along the Atlantic settled by colonists in the 1600s. Today, it had a picturesque quality thanks to restored historic homes, a restored historic downtown, and a hodgepodge of storefronts selling Irish pewter, falafel, and vegan gluten-free cupcakes.

In about ten more minutes and a little further south, they would be in Rye, a place where best-selling authors and cash-fat CEOs kept year-round homes and enjoyed some of the nicest, most expansive beaches in a state that only had thirteen miles of coastline.

No one talked for a few miles, and Augustus made sure he enjoyed the silence. He knew that being around these two females over the next two days wouldn't give him much of that.

"Have you ever been to The Montgomery?" Maggie asked him.

He wasn't much into small talk, but it was going to be a long weekend if he didn't at least try. Plus, it wouldn't look good if "Ian" wasn't talking to his fiancé. "The university held a few dinners there I was invited to."

"But did you go?"

"No time for things like that."

"Why do you have no time?"

"I have to work."

Maggie didn't have to waste breath on a follow-up. Roxie did it for her. "What's your work?"

Here it was. The point in a conversation with a child when he found out who the child was. And if he liked him or her afterward.

"I'm an entomologist."

"An et-no-what-oh?" the little girl asked.

"En-to-mol-o-gist. I study insects."

"You work with bugs?" There was disgust in her voice.

Oh goody, he thought. *Is she going to be an eww-er or a yuck-er?*

"I study them, dissect them, record them, and pretty much try to find out what makes them tick."

"Tick." The girl snorted out a laugh. She sounded just like her mother. "That's funny."

Somehow, he didn't think the state's moose population would feel that way. The unseasonably warm winters had made the tick population surge, meaning one moose could have up to 150,000 ticks on it, all of whom would be dining on its blood until the moose was too weak to find food.

The moose population was dying out because of those blood-thirsty parasites.

But that was information he kept to himself. The layperson didn't like to think about death, much less an insect the size of a pinhead causing it.

And the layperson definitely didn't like thinking about the guy studying the pinhead.

It gave them the heebie-jeebies.

"What's your favorite bug?" Roxie asked.

Now this was a line of questioning he appreciated. He looked in the rearview mirror to see the girl had big eyes and was leaning forward against her seatbelt. She seemed genuinely interested, and because of that, he didn't ignore the question.

"Right now, it's the *Culex pipiens.*"

"The Cu-what pi-huh?"

"The *Cu-lex pi-pi-ens.*" He stopped at a light, waiting to make the left that would take him toward Rye beaches and The Montgomery. "I'll give you a hint about what they are. They carry disease and looove to suuuck your bloooood."

He said this last part like he had lineage in Transylvania.

He waited, and when he didn't hear anything, he looked once more in his rearview mirror. The girl's forehead was wrinkled and she was brushing her stuffed animal's blue fuzzy arm across her mouth. Thinking.

Man, that *was* a Smurf! Seeing one took him back thirty years and Saturday morning cartoons.

Next to him, the redhead with the crazy wide mouth was clapping her hands. It made the air around her move, and she smelled like coconut. He liked coconut. But that didn't mean it would make him like the person wearing the coconut.

He wasn't that illogical.

"Ooh. Ooh. Pick me, pick me."

If he had Maggie Weston in his class, he would always be forgetting his place in his lectures. Not because of the coconut, but because of her smile. He answered her with a gruff, "And the answer would be what, Miss Weston?"

"Would that insect be a mosquito?"

"Why yes, it would be."

"Eww!" the girl whined in the back.

So. She was an eww-er.

He'd had such high hopes for Roxie, too.

Chapter Fourteen

"WE NEED A SUITE."

This was not good, not good at all.

"My mother told me that she had three suites and one room booked. I would like a suite." Maggie ignored the ocean views and the ocean breeze and the call of the seagulls just steps away. Instead, she was on her tiptoes, trying to look at the computer screen that was unhelpfully turned away from her. "We need two sleeping areas. One for me and my daughter and one for..." Her fiancé? Her boyfriend? Her friend? "One for him."

The girl behind the marble countertop moved her mouse, her eyes focused on the computer screen in front of her. Like she was making an effort to keep them there. "I have one suite booked for Abigail Weston, one for Peyton Wright, and one for Lauren Perfect. Our single goes to...Magdalene Weston."

Maggie was pissed. Once again, Peyton and Lauren

were fucking her over.

"Give me Peyton's or Lauren's room."

"They already checked in."

Shit and hell.

"Then let's book a second room." Augustus pointed to the "Pardon Our Dust" sign on the counter. "Do you have something available that hasn't been booked?"

"The rooms under renovation aren't safe for the public at the moment."

"I'm okay with bedspreads and artwork from the 1990s," Augustus said.

The girl, whose light blonde hair was tucked back into a low bun, gave them a long look, shifting her attention from one, then the other, then back again. She seemed to linger on Augustus a bit. "It flooded in that section of the hotel. Everything in that wing is pretty warped and damaged and smells like fish and mold."

The classical music piped throughout the lobby no longer relaxed Maggie. It had begun to sound like the kind of music that movies used right before a violent showdown.

"I know you, don't I?" Augustus asked the girl.

"Yes you do, Dr. Sloane." The clerk turned back to Maggie. She noticed the girl had ten vacant, lonely holes in the ear she could see. "The room booked for you is quite spacious, Miss Weston. It has a king-sized bed, a sleeper sofa, and a spot for a rollaway. Would you like a rollaway?"

Maggie was ready to answer that, yes, she would like one. But the girl's eyes were glued on the place where Maggie's arm touched Augustus's.

She sighed over the time-wasting moment. She didn't

pull away, though. Augustus didn't have cooties, she didn't have cooties. The end.

"Yes, a rollaway would be nice," Maggie replied. The girl barely registered her response.

The girl typed on her computer. "It's nice to have space. A lot of people make you crave space."

Augustus stepped closer to the desk, draping his forearms across the top until his hands hung down in the girl's area on the other side. "You're certain, Miss Adams, that you have no other rooms?" he asked, gesturing to the screen. "We would appreciate it if you could double check."

The girl most definitely gulped. "I'll double check," she whispered.

Fascinating. The Bug Dude made his students nervous.

Maggie got distracted when Roxie began pulling on her arm, needing to use the restroom. She pointed to the ladies' room, directly behind them, and Roxie took off, reciting to herself, "Don't pee, don't pee, don't pee."

Maggie turned back around, and that's when she saw the girl shaking as she picked up a print-out and stapled it to a map of the hotel.

"Did you take those notes I told you to?" Augustus was asking the girl.

"It's only been a day, Dr. Sloane." The girl blushed.

"But did you *start* taking notes?" Augustus pushed.

The girl's blushed deepened. "I went out with friends last night."

"Well that wasn't very wise, was it."

The girl's eyes narrowed and her mouth thinned as she studied her screen some more. This girl was young, Maggie thought. Definitely a student.

"I'm afraid we're one-hundred-percent booked up this weekend. I'm sorry, Dr. Sloane." Miss Adams didn't sound too sorry.

Maggie groaned and rested her forehead on the edge of the counter. Or, rather, on Augustus's hand that was on the edge of the counter. Whatever. She didn't care.

"Booked," Augustus said.

"Excuse me?"

"Booked. The place is booked. 'Up' is redundant."

Now it was time to intervene. Boy, didn't Augustus get that you caught more bees with honey?

Or would he rather kill the bees and study their innards? She jerked with a quick, silent laugh over her private joke.

She didn't feel like lifting her head yet. From where she was, she asked, "Mr. Sloane, could we wrap this up here? We have a pull-out sofa, a rollaway bed, and a real bed. We'll be okay."

"It's *Dr.* Sloane."

What she wanted to call him was Bugs. And not in the cute, "Eh, What's Up Doc?" way either.

But that would have to wait.

Because just then, a familiar and disliked voice said, "Well, well, well. Fancy meeting you here."

MAGGIE'S HEAD SNAPPED UP and she twisted around to face the two girls she had grown up with. They were her sisters biologically, but emotionally? They were people that Maggie didn't know or like that much. Maggie assumed it was because Peyton and Lauren were twins and ten years older.

A twin connection and a shared generation were sort of hard obstacles to overcome.

Peyton had her blonde hair tied back, black sunglasses in place, a fancy designer handbag hooked over her crooked elbow. Lauren had her blonde hair in soft waves that had taken hours to get that way, an expensive fleece vest on over the expensive long-sleeved workout shirt. Lauren's money, if memory served, was on a fancy money clip in her pocket, alongside her driver's license and credit cards.

It was such a guy thing to do, with a diva twist. Which totally went with Lauren.

She didn't get them, they didn't get her. And once a year, the two of them got together and had a girlfriend getaway. A spa trip to Phoenix, a walkabout in Australia, a week of Broadway musicals in Manhattan.

Without Maggie.

It was like their game of Ignore Maggie was still in effect. When Maggie was eight and they were eighteen, Peyton and Lauren pretended Maggie didn't exist for an entire month. They did it so well, they would ask one another over dinner if the other one wanted the "extra roll," which would be on Maggie's plate.

And now here they were, feet away from her.

"Hey." Maggie tried but she couldn't inject any kind of excitement into the word. Her hug for first Peyton and then Lauren followed suit. Their return hugs were just as lackluster. "Did you guys just get here?"

"Yeah. Sounds like you did, too." Peyton eyed Augustus. "*Dr.* Sloane, huh?"

Maggie looped her arm through Augustus's, and he took the hint. He tightened his own arm around it. It pulled her closer, against the side of his body. Against his very hard body. A little too close to his very hard body, in her opinion. She put a hand up as if she were steadying herself, but she was really pushing herself away a bit.

She couldn't think straight if she was this close to all that hard…stuff.

"Yes, this is Dr. Sloane." And to make the most out of the moment, she added, "This is *my* Dr. Sloane."

Peyton raised an eyebrow. Okay, maybe Maggie had overdone it just the tiniest bit. She changed the topic. "The itinerary Mom emailed us said that there's a cruise at 3:00?"

"Pound back the Dramamine now," Peyton said knowingly.

"Do you get seasick then?" Augustus asked. He pulled her even closer. And she got to feel even more of his body.

"A little." Damn. It was a good body. When did the Bug Dude have time to increase his lean body mass?

A little?" Peyton mocked. "Imagine a volcano. It's erupting. But instead of lava, it's vomit. Getting on everyone."

Maggie tightened her hold on Augustus's arm. He reciprocated, and she got pulled too close again. This time, she decided it wasn't such a bad thing. "It got on you and Lauren. That's not *everyone*." Once and only once had she gotten sea sick, back when she was ten and her sisters were twenty. It was a tour of the Florida coastline, and it lasted for eight hours.

For seven of those hours, she couldn't keep down food, water, or spit.

Personally, Maggie thought her sisters had deserved it. Pretending she hadn't existed for a month had been pure evil.

In Maggie's opinion, a little vomit had absolved them of that sin.

But only that one sin.

There were a lot more sins Maggie hadn't forgiven yet.

"Where's Roxie?" Lauren asked.

Maggie let the subject change. This was one reason why Lauren was the sister she liked slightly more. She was just a little bit smarter at reading a room compared to Peyton.

"She's in the restroom." Which meant this was a good time to introduce Augustus. "This is Augustus Sloane. These two are my sisters, Peyton and Lauren."

"I thought you told Mom his name was Ian?" Lauren asked.

"Yeah. Mom said his name was Ian," Peyton argued.

Oh hell. Maggie had been reminding herself all morning to call him Ian, and what was the first thing she did?

Didn't call him Ian, that's what.

Augustus tried to help her out of her blunder. "Ian is my given name, but I prefer my middle name."

"You prefer Augustus to Ian?" Peyton asked, the signature Weston Woman eyebrow up, doubt lacing her words.

"Yes, I do. Augustus was an emperor, after all."

Peyton adjusted her handbag and gave Maggie a look.

Maggie knew that look. *I'm supposed to be jealous of you with this guy. C'mon!*

"Where'd you get this guy, Maggie?" Lauren asked. "Has he been trapped on some glacier, studying penguins at the North Pole or something?"

"South Pole," Augustus interjected.

"Excuse me?" Peyton said in her best *No he di'int* voice.

"Penguins are erroneously believed to be at the North Pole, with Santa and Rudolph. But they are, in fact, at the South Pole."

"Um, okay," Peyton said, rolling her eyes at her younger twin. Lauren returned the favor.

Luckily, Augustus was spared intense interrogation when Roxie joined them. The Twins turned on their smiles and their high-pitched oohs and ahhs as they admired their niece.

Maggie felt a sharp pain in her stomach, and she massaged it, pretending she didn't know what was causing it, especially on a day when she'd had no coffee.

So this was what it felt like to stumble into a snake pit with no antidote.

There was squealing and hugging and saying "You are *so* big!" for the next five minutes.

Maggie took that moment to make sure she had everything she needed: the keys to the room, the WiFi password, and a detailed map of where everything was: pool, workout room, vending machines, laundry.

They were only staying a night, but Maggie liked to be prepared for anything that could come her way.

Including the shit she knew her family was about to put her through.

MAGGIE WAS SUCH AN IDIOT. She had been prepared for dealing with the Weston family.

She hadn't prepared herself to deal with the Allen family, too.

Roxie's father's family.

"C'mon, Maggie." Alex Whelan was on the other end of her cellphone. He had been her weak moment, a man made up of tattoos and motorcycles and two-day stubble. A man of her dreams, she'd convinced herself.

No one had warned her that he was also made up of heartbreak and distrust .

"You've got to let me have Rox for just an hour," he told her over the phone.

Room 543 faced the ocean, a beautiful, peaceful view. Maggie had only been in the room ten minutes when her phone rang and her ex reminded her by the end of his first sentence about why he was her ex.

And the peace of the room and this location? Shot all

to shit.

"I don't *gotta* do anything, Alex. I have full custody of Roxie, which means I don't have to even let her see you. But I do. You call, you give me a day and time, and I make sure you see her. But Mother's Day? Are ya nuts?" Maggie tried to lighten the tone this conversation had taken on, especially with Roxie in earshot, but it was hard. So, so hard.

A long time ago, Maggie had accepted her role as Roxie's full-time parent and Alex as her part-time plaything. But Alex was not supposed to show his face anywhere near Roxie or her when it was Maggie's *day*. Her *weekend*. Hell, her *month*.

And in July, when it was Maggie's birthday, the same rules applied.

"But Mom is having all the grandkids here and the only one missing is Rox."

"Why didn't you tell me about it sooner?"

Silence. And then: "I forgot."

The infuriating thing was, even though she wanted to tell him no, Maggie also saw the practicality of the situation. Most of Helen's grandkids lived either in New Hampshire, Maine, or Massachusetts, but two lived in Toronto and never came down.

And Helen was 79 and had a pacemaker and Stage 2 breast cancer. Time was not her friend.

"When is the photo shoot?" she said, her teeth gritted.

"At six, over at Abbott Farm. It's two minutes from you, Mags."

"I'm not in Maple Woods. It's an hour from where we are right now."

"Where the hell are you guys?"

Maggie shut her eyes and dug her fingers into her forehead, massaging the headache that was building there.

Trust Alex to be pissed over nothing.

One reason behind why she hadn't ever thought, for one second, that she would ever tether herself to him with wedding vows.

No, instead you tethered yourself to him with a human being.

Luckily, the human being was worth it.

"Can you do it, Maggie? Mom would love it if Rox came. Even you. She always liked you."

Ten minutes later, Maggie hung up the phone, picked up a pillow, smothered her face, and screamed.

Shit and hell and everything in between!

"I'm thinking that call wasn't a good call."

She peeled her face from the pillow. Augustus stood next to the bed, holding a garment bag and a matching black leather toiletry kit. He looked like a damn model for something manly. Like for a cologne. Or boxer briefs. Or steak.

"Nope. Not a good call at all." She told him about the photo shoot. "So not only do I get to be all seasick on a boat today, but I then have to see my ex." She threw the pillow into the air a bit and punched it down onto the bed. "I have to see my ex this weekend of all weekends. *My* weekend."

"*Your* weekend?" Augustus set his black toiletry bag down and pulled out his toothbrush and toothpaste. "You've called dibs on the entire weekend?"

"All mothers have called dibs on this weekend. We've earned this weekend."

"Last I heard, you got a day. I think that's quite fair."

Maggie fell back onto the bed. "Oh, if life was fair, we'd get the whole damn year. Every single day, children would bring their mothers breakfast in bed and say please and thank you and do their own laundry."

When she didn't hear anything, she opened her eyes. He was still there, but he was focused on unpacking.

Augustus had turned over a glass tumbler and had stood his toothbrush and toothpaste in it. He was currently hanging a white shirt on a hanger. The kind that was an undershirt.

"You hang up underwear?" she deadpanned.

"And you *don't* hang up underwear?" he replied back.

She didn't hang up anything, not when she would be here for less than twenty-four hours.

Maggie fell back on the king-sized bed, her head bouncing against the mattress. "You are one weird dude."

The door to the bathroom opened and Roxie came out, closing the door behind her and looking timid. Something was up.

"Are you feeling okay, LaLa?"

"Yeah. I--." She reached for the room's remote. "Can I watch TV?"

Maggie didn't pressure her to give her details. She'd wait until later, when they didn't have an audience.

"Just stay away from anything with adult themes, any news, and HBO. And if one of those sad abused animal commercials come on, you know, the ones where the dogs and cats have their fur burned off and their eyeballs are hanging out, turn those off too."

Augustus added his one cent. "Maybe it would be easier to tell her what she *could* watch rather than what she *couldn't.*"

Maggie twisted on the bed, rolling to one side, then the next, trying to work out the kinks that were only going to get worse as this weekend went on. "I'm sure that if it was up to you, you wouldn't let her watch TV at all."

Augustus put his green-and-navy-blue striped tie on the back of a chair. "I didn't watch TV growing up."

"Was it too pedantic for you?"

He paused in his travels to and from the closet. "No, but nice use of the word. We didn't watch TV because we didn't own one."

"Too poor?" Maggie guessed.

"Too busy. Traveling to London and Prague and Bruges and Paris and Barcelona."

"Tough life." She pushed up onto her elbows. "Those don't sound like military deployments. There's always a shitty base thrown in there, like South Korea or Topeka, Kansas. None of those places are the least bit shitty." She spied the coffee maker next to Augustus's toothbrush set-up. She went over and started making a pot.

It was going to be a long-ass day. And her stomach was feeling okay.

She was willing to take her chances with coffee in return for the energy boost. And she'd water it down with tons of creamer.

Yeah, that was the ticket.

"My father was a doctor for quite a few predominant families."

"Anyone I know?" She put in a filter and dumped in a package of coffee.

As she filled the tank with water, she began to think that this is how a drug addict must feel when trying to score his next hit.

Augustus was naming off actors and presidents and queens when she tuned back in to what he was saying.

"Wow. Tough life." The phone rang next to the bed. Maggie answered it before she remembered not to. That she needed a breather after the Alex call. "Speak."

There was a brief silence. "Am I a dog?" she heard her mother ask.

Maggie winced.

The Weekend from Hell was officially up and running.

Chapter Sixteen

AN HOUR LATER, MAGGIE STOOD with her mom and her sisters on the upper deck of the Lorna Lune. Her wide-brimmed hat felt too tight on her head, and her blue-and-white striped scarf was strangling her.

Then again, the company she was keeping might have had something to do with feeling attacked.

"You should really get Roxie into a math league program. A girl's math scores start deteriorating from fourth grade on," Peyton was saying.

"And I noticed she likes her sugar," Lauren whispered not so quietly. "You should get her on a fitness program before her cute baby pudge turns into full-blown obesity."

"Didn't you tell me Ian was working on her weight?" her mother asked.

Maggie shook her head slowly, wondering if she was going insane. Why was her mother making up stuff? "No, I didn't."

"And his name is Augustus, Mom." Peyton's signature eyebrow went up. "You would think Maggie would know the guy's name."

"I told you already. Another Ian joined his department. To limit confusion, he's going by Augustus now." It was a small lie, but it was one that was going to save the bigger lie.

Speaking of…Augustus stood slightly apart from the four women, a glass of ginger ale in his hand, a white button-down shirt tucked into black dress pants. He was wearing his tie, too.

He looked pretty good, she had to admit.

Sure, he seemed a little distracted, like he had mosquitoes on the brain, but Maggie wasn't expecting perfection. Him just being here, looking like that and having a doctor title, was turning out to be more than enough.

She'd already caught Peyton checking him out twice when she thought no one was looking.

Everyone was on the first level of the boat, where it was enclosed, because the ocean breeze was pretty dang cold. The five kids were also inside, fighting over the one set of high-powered binoculars welded to the inside deck.

Hayden was trying to push Roxie out of the way, but her baby wasn't some wisp of an eight-year-old. She liked her ice cream and her licorice and still had some baby pudge, as Lauren so delicately put it.

But that pudge was helping Rox stand her ground against the older but skinnier kid.

Maggie watched the action going down with a smile and with no need to intervene. Plus, she was still procrastinating from telling her mom about the 6 o'clock photo shoot with Grandma Helen.

When her Lauren and Peyton decided to intervene with the kids a few minutes later, Maggie saw that she had no more excuses to put off the inevitable.

"Hey Mom." She came up behind the small woman in her Chanel jacket and costume pearls. Her hair was dyed brown, her lips were tattooed pink, and her trim figure was rigorously managed through hot lemon water and salads.

"Magdalene." She put her hands out. Not for a hug, though. More for a quick grab, pull in, and kiss the air next to Maggie's face.

"Thanks for taking us all out today, Mom. That was beyond generous of you."

"It's just money. I have it. I spend it. The end." Her mother, as usual, was starting a fight when there was nothing to fight about.

"And we appreciate that," Maggie said. Time to rip the Band-Aid off, short hairs and all. "I have to duck out with Roxie at around 5 o'clock." Deep breath. It was time to take the hill. "Grandma Helen is having a little photo shoot she wants Roxie at."

Her mother smoothed an imaginary wrinkle from the sleeve of her blazer. "All right."

Of everything Abigail Weston could have said, this would not have made it into Maggie's Top 100 Guesses.

"All right then," Maggie agreed.

Oh hell.

If her mother wasn't going to lay into her now, that meant the fun and games would come later.

Awesome.

"HEY."

Even without looking, Augustus knew it was Roxie. Her little girl voice had such an air of…command…behind it. He looked up from his Blackberry and an email about a student needing an extension because his grandmother was dying.

Not *dead* but *dying*. As grandmothers conveniently did at finals. He had already tapped out his reply: *No postponements allowed. Sorry about Grandma. –A.S.*

He hit send and put his phone away. "You having fun, kid?"

She shrugged. She was still dressed all in blue, but he had a feeling this wasn't a one-time occurrence. "It's all relative."

He couldn't stop his smile. "Do you even know what that means?"

"That there are worse things and better things. It's all in how I look at it."

"Your mom tell you that?"

"It's one of her favorite sayings."

His opinion of Maggie Weston inched up the smallest bit. He liked it when kids understood the kind of world they lived in. He thought too many parents shielded their children for way too long. To their detriment, too.

"So who are you?" Roxie asked.

Ah. Now they were getting to the reason for this conversation. "A friend."

"I know that. But what *kind* of friend?

And now he understood why parents shielded their

kids. It meant they had fewer headaches as they avoided having to explain incredibly complex concepts. "I'm a guy friend."

"Mom already has one of those. He's my dad. His name is Alex." She lowered her voice. "She doesn't like him too much."

"Then that's not a friend."

"Why?"

Was this girl even listening to what she was saying? "Because she doesn't like him."

"I knew it!" She sounded victorious.

"I'm just repeating what you said, kid."

"Oh." She pulled out her ponytail and redid her hair. Behind her, her cousins were split into two groups: the girls were playing with each other's hair, and the boys were playing with someone's iPhone.

The division of the sexes was typical and unsurprising. But this girl in her blue outfit and her adult conversations was...surprising.

Having Maggie Weston as a mom had helped this kid.

Where did that come from? he wondered.

"Why are you here with us?" Roxie was asking. "My mom likes my dad. She touches his arm sometimes. You don't do stuff like that if you don't like someone."

No, he wasn't Roxie's dad. He was no one's dad because he didn't want that kind of life. He didn't think he ever would.

He realized the kid had asked him a question he hadn't answered yet: *Why was he here?* Augustus could've played along with Maggie's pretense, that he was Ian the Fiancé, but that would have taken too much energy and brain space, two commodities he saved for where he needed it most: his work.

And so he settled on: "Because she told her family she was engaged, and I happened to be in the right place at the right time.

Roxie gaped at him. "You're engaged to my mom?"

"No." The girl visibly relaxed, her shoulders slumping, her breath exhaling. He was already digging himself an early grave. He'd just dig it a little deeper. "We're just saying that I am."

She quirked an eyebrow at him. It was fairly good, too. She definitely had the Weston gene. "That's crazysauce," she said dramatically.

"Trust me, kid. I know."

Chapter Seventeen

Maggie. Hey. You're probably busy doing something fun. When you're done with that and you're like, "Hey, I wonder how I could have some more fun," give me a call.

MAGGIE SMILED as she stood on a slope at Abbott Farm, Roxie posing with her cousins next to a wagon holding hay and apples. She listened to the voicemail for a third time, still smiling.

Fisher, Noah Fisher, had just called. The man from The Coffee Pot, who had told her the bus had already come and gone.

How had he gotten her number?

But she sort of knew. Maple Woods was small, and she knew her landlord also owned the lease on the coffee shop, too. People talked, and they talked about other people when they were bored.

She wasn't too worried about how Fisher, Noah Fisher, had gotten her number. She was just happy that she had a guy leaving her a cute message.

Not that it could go anywhere. She wasn't in that kind of headspace with that kind of time. *Says the girl who's with a guy she rented.*

But she had to admit, listening to Noah's message made her almost forget being cold and getting colder. And how her stomach was feeling bad and getting worse.

Stupid coffee.

Stupid her for not eating anything with her coffee and for thinking her stomach would be on a break from torturing her.

But she ignored the stomachache and instead thought about the voicemail, one of the few bright spots from this weekend.

Her weekend. Which had not been about her at all.

Maggie, this isn't about you. Stop being such a selfish crank. You're healthy and you're with your daughter. The end.

"Good message?"

She looked up to see Augustus with his hands in his pockets, leaning against a tree, his light brown eyes on her. But not in any sort of dreamy way.

He was being every inch the scientist inspecting his specimen.

"Just listening to a nice person. Not too many of those around today." She saved the message before putting the phone back in the pocket of her light jacket. She zipped it up, preparing for the drop in temperature that was about to happen once the sun was 100-percent down.

She looked up when she heard Roxie laugh. If the Weston cousins were the bad ones, these cousins were definitely the good ones. They liked to fish and hunt and go ATVing, and they liked to listen to their parents and say please and thank you.

The photographer had finished taking formal pictures and was now snapping candids of the kids sticking out their tongues and jumping in the air and pretending they were all taking a bow.

Maggie had already asked for the woman's business card. Jessa had talked about having a photographer at Jamison's party tomorrow. When Jessa saw the price sheet on such a service, she'd nip that dream in the bud.

Maggie listened to the giggles and shrieks and closed her eyes, relaxed for the first time all day. She breathed in the spring evening. The air was chilly, but at least the winter snow had disappeared. Yes, it had left behind the kind of mud that could suck a shoe off. But she'd take mud over snow. It had been a super-long winter, with too many snow days that had kept the busses off the roads and the kids out of school for too long. They would all be lucky if school and all the make-up days ended in July.

The long winter had made Roxie fussy, and it had made Maggie long for a change of scenery.

Be careful what you wish for.

She was now in Maple Woods, trying to unpack in between work and parenting and facing a super-nutty summer: Roxie being underfoot, a humongous fortieth birthday party for Jessa (if Jessa liked how Jamison's party turned out), and her 15-year class reunion.

Not that she was worried about the class reunion. She looked better than she had in high school, when she had worn braces and an extra forty pounds thanks to too many red Zingers.

She looked over at her Rent-a-Man. The one thing she didn't have in time for the reunion was a male companion. The idea of having a cute guy with her appealed to her.

And Augustus *was* cute…when he wasn't frowning over his Blackberry, working out some kind of silent problem that only his entomologist brain could fathom.

She could always save the money and take Alex.

She pinched herself hard. Real hard. *Are ya nuts?*

She could maybe take Noah Fisher. *One cute text does not mean you can invite him to fly to Florida and pose as your guy.*

Then again, his voicemail *had* said to call him after she was done having her fun. Well, this weekend hadn't been fun at all. She was more than ready to call and make that date.

But she knew that she couldn't do it here, with so many ears around with mouths that would report back to Alex and LaLa. And so she had to be content with feeling like a kid waiting for Christmas morning.

And it felt lovely.

That was until her stomach made a hard twist. She swayed and bumped into Augustus. His hand reached out to steady her.

"Are you okay?"

"It's been a long day, that's all." She tried to act like she was fine, that she was overwhelmed with thoughts of Noah Fisher.

But she knew the truth. She had been fighting the truth for about six months now. She had been living with stress for too long, and now her body was trying to make sure she knew she was paying for it.

She needed to gauge just how bad she was. She put her hand out in front of her but down low, so that Augustus couldn't quite figure out what she was doing. But she wasn't fooling anyone.

"Why is your hand shaking, Maggie?"

She tried playing it off. "It's hard to control myself when I'm around you," she joked.

"Uh huh." He grabbed her hand. "You're freezing, and it's not that cold out." The scowl deepened. "Why are you so cold?"

She really didn't have the energy to give an in-depth explanation. Instead, she said, "I just need get some Tums."

Maggie glanced over at Roxie, who was playing some sort of How-Far-Can-I-Throw-This-Rock game with a couple of cousins. She couldn't take her daughter away from that. Maggie was her mom and her friend, but she couldn't be ten cousins that teased and rough housed and made her belly hurt from non-stop laughter.

Seeing her like this, Maggie couldn't cut Roxie's visit short. This hand shaking business would go away. If it didn't, she'd take a handful of Tums when she got back to the room and then go to the hotel pool and have Roxie dive for the plastic eggs she had brought, filled with rocks and coins.

Then she had about four hours of work ahead of her, but she could work on it while Roxie slept.

Then she had to jog on the treadmill in the hotel's gym.

It was a full night, but she could manage a few more minutes here. She had managed for months. Then she'd eat her Tums and get back on schedule.

It was a good plan.

It just wasn't what ended up happening.

Chapter Eighteen

MAGGIE MOANED. Her stomach was mad at her, real mad.

Maggie curled up into a tighter ball, barely feeling the carpet under her. She squeezed her knees into her chest, and she rocked and moaned, rocked and moaned.

Her neck was cool and wet, and she had no idea why and no energy to figure it out.

Augustus squatted next to her, taking a washcloth from her neck and replacing it with the white one in his hand.

"How long have you had stomach pains?" Augustus had his phone in his hands and was typing into it.

"No idea, Bugs." She had some idea. But she was in too much pain to go into the details. Details took too much effort.

"Bugs," he repeated. "Is that supposed to be a putdown?"

"Bugs. Like in Bunny. Like in what you do." The last

word came out with a moan. "Or it's because you're bugging the shit out of me."

He ignored her and read off his phone. "Do you have a history with gallstones?" he asked.

"No." *Groan.*

"Appendix?"

"No."

"Female cramping?"

Groooooannnnn. "I pushed a kid out of my vagina eight years ago. I think I can handle menstrual cramps."

"Didn't want to leave a stone unturned, Maggie."

There was a break in the pain. She used it to say, "Where's Rox?"

"With her cousins. I told her you more than likely had eaten something that disagree with you and needed to defecate."

A lot of women would be embarrassed. Not Maggie. She was in too much pain.

"Do I need to call an ambulance?"

"No!" Her line of work didn't come with insurance, and Roxie was on her dad's insurance. The ambulance alone would be a thousand bucks. "I've had this before. It'll pass. I just have to eat a shitload of Tums and stop drinking coffee."

He continued looking at his phone, scrolling. Presumably searching for answers. Or checking his e-mail. "Why did you drink so much coffee today if you knew it disagreed with you?"

"I love the stuff, and I lapsed and binged. Okay?"

"Okay." He put his phone away. "I can get you some Tums if you'd like."

"Please."

There was a knock on their suite door. Bugs left her and went down the small hall to the door that was out of sight.

"Hello Mrs. Weston."

Oh, hell and shit and shit and hell.

"How is Magdalene?"

She hoped to hell that Bugs knew he had to be her buffer. She didn't have the energy to open her eyes or say a word to her mother at this moment.

"It's her stomach, isn't it." Her mother sounded so damn sure of herself. Maggie curled herself even tighter. The fetal position was such an underrated coping mechanism.

"I brought one of the kid's organic chocolate milk thingies. Thought it could help Magdalene's tummy. It did when she was little and had one of these...episodes."

There was silence, and Maggie almost called out to her mom. It might be nice to have her here, holding her hand, as she rode the waves of pain.

"Do you know what she has, Mrs. Weston?"

Oh Mom, keep your mouth shut. No one needs to know. Especially Bugs. He'll just look at me like I'm even stupider than Mister Ph.D.-Slash-M.D. thinks I am.

"She's always been a little lactose intolerant."

If Maggie wasn't feeling so cruddy, she would have called her mom in here. Because her mom was spinning fairytales.

"And so you brought her milk?" Bugs asked.

"Oh. Well, maybe it was something else she couldn't tolerate. I just know the milk helped."

There was a silence, and Maggie could almost see

Bugs calmly waiting for her mother to explain herself and to sort through the confusion.

She didn't, though.

Bugs took the hint and moved the conversation along. "That's thoughtful of you, Abigail. I'll make sure she gets it."

There was a pause that felt long to Maggie. She briefly wondered who was winning the staring contest.

Or maybe Bugs had shut the door with no goodbye and was now checking his phone.

As weak and sick as she was, Maggie smiled at that thought. She was starting to feel better. Still like shit, but she didn't think she'd die if she had to move.

And then she heard Augustus say, "Maggie needs some rest right now, Mrs. Weston. I know Roxie's in Lauren's room. Can you ask them if she can spend the night there?"

Augustus said something else and Abigail said something back but Maggie was no longer invested in the conversation. She was too busy moving the washcloth from her neck to her cheeks to her forehead and worrying about Roxie spending the night with the Bad Cousins.

And then the rag was being tugged out of her hands. She followed it blindly, trying to keep the rag on her too-hot skin. Why was the rag being so mean to her?

"It's okay, Maggie," Bugs said. "I'm just going to run this under some cold water again." But he didn't leave her side like she thought he would. Instead, she felt herself being lifted from the ground.

"I'm too heavy," she groaned. It seemed like the thing to say.

"Shut up." He laid her down on a soft mattress and cool fabric touched her hot skin. Then she felt a straw slip between her lips. Bugs had the milk in front of her. "Drink."

She sipped. "You're being awfully good to me, Bugs."

"You bought and paid for me. It's the least I can do." He stayed squatted next to her as she drank the milk, his one hand holding the container, his other hand adjusting the rag on her neck.

The attention felt good. Real good.

No one had taken care of her for months. Years.

Maybe even a full decade.

Maggie finished the milk and asked, "Can I tell you something Bugs?"

He grunted and she took that as a *yes.*

"I paid for you with a check that's post-dated for Monday."

"A lot of people do that."

She snorted. "Yeah, well, I do it a lot. It's the bane of living check to check."

"I hear many people do that."

She looked out the double doors at the ocean beyond. This room was so beautiful, and this setting was surreal. It was so far removed from her day-to-day world of taking care of her daughter and keeping a roof over their heads.

"I don't want to be 'many' people. I want to be that parent who makes enough to send my kid to dance class. To send her to gymnastics. To send her to an art camp for winter break, to a soccer camp for spring break, to some sleep-away camp for summer break."

"Not a lot of people can give their kids all those

things, Maggie." His hand stayed on the washcloth, keeping it in place on her neck. It was warm. She was warm. Why was she so warm?

"I just don't feel like I'm doing right by my kid. I'm allowed to feel that, okay?"

"You're allowed to feel that way, but you're not allowed to make yourself feel like less of a person because of it."

Out in the hallway a cart rolled by—housekeeping? room service?—reminding her she wasn't in her apartment. That Roxie wasn't just feet away, listening to every word and every sound.

Reminding her that she was alone with a man for the first time in a long, long, long time.

A no-strings guy that you paid for, she reminded herself.

"Bugs?"

"Really? You're going to keep using that name?"

"Let a sick woman have her way." She was feeling less sick, but she'd keep that to herself for now.

He put his fingers up to her forehead. "Fine. Enjoy it while you can, Curly."

"Curly? Like in Moe and Larry?"

"You gave me a nickname. I thought I'd return the favor."

"And you could only come up with Curly? That's not very creative, Doctor."

"I could call you Heterochromia."

The technical term for her differently colored eyes. "That's not very creative."

"Chromia for short?"

She just gave him a look.

"Curly it is then."

They didn't say anything else, and Maggie realized for the first time that the room was very dark. Only the hall light was on.

Bugs sat next to her, the empty milk carton in his one hand, a washcloth pressed against her nape with the other.

"I think I like you, Bugs."

He snorted. "What do you want?"

"I want to say that I think that I like you." She tried to push herself up onto an elbow, but the motion tweaked her stomach. She laid back down. "I want Roxie."

"She's with her cousins."

"They're assholes."

"But they're all with your sister. Give her a little wiggle room, okay?"

Wiggle room. Maggie didn't do that real well. She was too used to being mother, father, friend, warden, playmate, provider, nurse...

But who was she when she wasn't a mom or a party planner?

When she wasn't raising her daughter or keeping a roof over their heads?

She wanted to know. Right now, she wanted to know.

And that's when the thought popped into her head.

It was an insane thought. A weird thought at the very least.

But she liked weird. Weird moments made her forget the day-to-day problems with reality. Oddly enough, weird moments helped remind her to be happy.

"Bugs?"

"Yes, Curly. What is it?"

She just wanted to feel normal, as if she had no worries in the world. No responsibilities. Just for a tiny moment.

A Maggie moment.

"How would you feel about kissing me?"

 *Chapter Nineteen*

OF EVERYTHING MAGGIE WESTON could have said, this was probably Number 12 on the list in Augustus's head.

Yes, he had a list. After Dot had asked him to be a part of this weekend, he had picked up sushi at The Store Basket and took a break from mosquitos as he worked on probabilities.

Specifically, he worked through the odds of what would happen when a woman who didn't date was given a weekend with a male she had "rented."

So *her* asking *him* if he would kiss her was Number 12.

Number 11? *Him* asking *her* for the kiss.

Number 1 had been asking if *he* could see *her* naked.

He wasn't a jerk or a pervert to come up with this list. He had been honest with himself while using precedents seen in the animal kingdom. Wild animals, after all, weren't as big into kissing as humans were.

Not as much as they were into penis on vagina

contact.

"Did you pay for kissing?" he asked. When her face started to flush red, he backed off the teasing. "I'm kidding, Maggie. This 'rent-a-man' situation is a novelty to me. I hope you know that. I don't need the money, and to tell you the truth, Dotty and Dolly aren't even paying me."

"Then why are you doing it?"

"I owe them." He left it at that. No one knew about the deal he had made with Dot.

Or had it been Dolly?

He heard her legs shift under the sheets, and across from him, the air conditioner rattled. Kissing was an interesting ritual. Ten percent of the world didn't kiss, but there was a belief that those cultures that did only did so because they were trying to derive the kind of comfort they had found while being breastfed.

He had not been breastfed, but he still enjoyed a good kiss.

And he had a feeling that his kiss with Curly would be really, really good.

MAGGIE PUSHED up onto her elbows and let the sheet slip to her waist. She was still in her clothes from the day, a slouchy sweater with red-and-white stripes. She let it fall over one shoulder.

She ran a hand through her curls, fluffing air through the roots. "So?" she asked.

"I'm running through the numbers."

She tipped her head back and groaned. "God, Bugs,

you can be so friggin' annoy—"

That's all she got out because his lips were on hers.

They were soft lips, and they tasted like bergamot from the Earl Grey tea he had brewed in the room after her ill-chosen coffee. They were soft lips, but they were talented lips, too. They tasted her top lip, her bottom lip, the stuff in between her lips.

Okay, that hadn't been a sexy thought. Think sexy, think sexy, Maggie repeated to herself.

But, wow, she couldn't turn her brain off. She could hear feet pounding in the hallway, the wind rustling outside through her open balcony door, muffled voices and gunshots playing from a TV next door.

Maggie pulled back from the sexy-ass man sharing a king-sized bed with her, in a room with no child in it, in a hotel worth more than anything she could save up anytime soon.

The sexy-ass man followed her, his eyes half-hooded, looking like sex on toast.

There were right times and right places.

This was the right place.

But the wrong time. Her head just wasn't in the right spot.

"Bugs?"

He didn't say a word. But he stayed close, watching her lips, breathing on them, he was so close.

"Do you have any quarters?" she whispered.

"I think so?"

"I'm craving a Twinkie. Or a Snowball. Can you get me something cakey with cream inside?"

He didn't say anything at first. Then he smiled. It was small and it only partly reached his eyes, but it was there. "Maybe," he said.

"And Roxie? Can you go get her?"

He lifted an eyebrow but he nodded.

"Sure."

"Thanks." Maggie didn't say anything about the kiss and neither did Bugs.

Instead, he walked to the tumbler sitting next to the one holding his toothbrush. Metal tinkled against glass as he started fishing out coins.

Maggie was impressed.

Bugs knew how to do no-strings like a pro.

Chapter Twenty

"HAPPY MOTHER'S DAY to you, Happy Mother's Day to youuuuu…."

Maggie opened her eyes. Pale, early morning light filled the window-lined room. Roxie stood by the side of her bed, holding a white cup with steam rising from it. Behind her was Bugs, putting his room key on the hotel's dresser.

"Happy Mother's Day dear Mommy, Happy Mother's Day tooooooo yooooouuuu."

Maggie scooted up, the sheets a mess to her right where Roxie had slept next to her. The hotel clock said it was 5:42 a.m.

"Thank you, LaLa." She carefully took the cup. She sniffed.

"Hot chocolate?" she guessed.

"We didn't think coffee would be a good idea," Bugs said.

"But I got you the white hot chocolate with two

squirts of almond syrup," Roxie was quick to add.

"Someone's been listening to me at the Starbucks drive-thru." Maggie gave the little girl a raspberry on the temple. Roxie giggled but didn't pull away. If anything, she pushed herself into Maggie. Maggie gave her another raspberry before she took a sip and sighed. "Perfect."

"I know," Roxie said.

"How did you get there?"

Roxie pointed at Augustus. "Him. I told him I needed to get you a present and he took me." She lifted a paper bag off the bed. "And pound cake. I know that you love their pound cake."

"I sure do." She opened the bag and sniffed. "And that is some good-smelling pound cake."

"She bought it all with her own money, too," Augustus said, a note of humor in his voice. "Most of it was pennies, but they were all hers."

Maggie thought about the nearest Starbucks in this area. "You really drove an hour roundtrip to get this?" she asked him.

He shrugged. "I had to earn my keep, so I did."

Maggie took a drink. It really did taste like the way she always ordered it. "Little Me," she said to Roxie, "you did well."

"I know."

Maggie felt tears in her eyes and she pressed a long, hard kiss onto Roxie's forehead.

The girl gave a goofy grin and fell into her mother, who promptly gave her another raspberry.

Chapter Twenty-One

"DID YOU TRY THE LEMON MOUSSE?"

"A bite."

"The cherry Chambord chocolates?"

"A bite."

"The turtle cake?"

"Two bites."

"You are a model of moderation," Bugs said, forking another heaping forkful of chocolate and chocolate ganache and homemade whipped cream into his mouth. It was his fifth dessert. His fifth completed dessert, too.

"What I am is a person with a bad tummy." Maggie leaned back in her chair, her hand over her stomach. The pain had started up again. It wasn't as bad as it had been, but it was there.

She'd have to see someone, and soon.

Just as soon as she got herself insured.

Augustus looked at her plate, even as he was

shoveling in another bite of food. Maggie pushed the pile of desserts at him. "Have at it."

At least one of them should fully enjoy the $129-per-person brunch.

Maggie shook her head as she watched Bugs inhale each sweet with a look of utter bliss. Who would've thought Mr. Entomologist would be weak when it came to sugar?

Her mother's voice broke through her thoughts. She was holding court a few chairs away, and entertaining four of her five grandchildren.

Roxie wasn't there or anywhere in current sight. Maggie looked around, curious but not panicked. Roxie knew to stay in eyeshot. Sure enough, she stood at the chocolate fondue, mesmerized with the way the chocolate flowed over a fork in her hand.

Watching her daughter investigate the ways of the world, Maggie was content. Her stomach hurt, she had a party to work tonight, and she was sitting next to a man she had paid to be there, but that didn't take away from what this weird but wonderful moment was.

Happy.

"WHEN'S THE BIG DAY?"

Lauren sat down in the empty chair next to Maggie's. The table shook as she set her elbow on the white cloth, her head on her hand. Her eyes were at half-mast.

Lauren had apparently been sampling the bottomless mimosas. Which meant this conversation was going to be…probing.

Maggie started the inevitable. "We haven't really talked about—"

"February." Bugs stated the lie easily as he gestured to a passing waitress to refill his water glass.

"February? Didn't that month already pass?" Lauren's blood alcohol content was definitely starting to show.

"The February that occurs next year." He said the words slowly. He appeared to realize that he wasn't talking to someone who was all there.

What was Bugs doing? It was one thing to create a pretense to get through a weekend. But why create a pretense the would go into next year?

She leaned into him, smiling for Lauren's benefit. And she whispered, "Bugs, what the fuck are you doing?"

He drank his water and raised his eyebrows, but at least he didn't say anything else.

"I can't believe a guy finally nailed you down," Lauren gloated. "Job well done, Augustus. Job well done indeed."

Bugs didn't respond to Lauren.

Maggie's nails in his thigh had probably made him think twice.

 Chapter Twenty-Two

"WHY DID YOU SAY THAT?"

Maggie shifted on the massage table until her head felt more comfortable in the donut-shaped headpiece, her nose and mouth comfortably centered in the opening.

"Excuse me?" The woman digging an elbow into Maggie's shoulder blade dug a little less deeply.

"I was talking to my guy over there. Keep doing that wonderful thing you're doing. And if I scream a little, it's a good scream. Just keep going." Maggie's knots had their own knots. Pain was going to be a good thing for the next pre-paid hour.

Bugs still hadn't responded. She tried again. "Augustus!"

"Wha?" He sounded like he was half-asleep.

"Did you go to sleep?"

"Not with you screaming at me."

"I'm not screaming. I raised my voice so you knew I

was talking to you."

"Well, good work. I know you're talking to me." His voice got a little clearer. And a little louder. "Now talk."

She wanted to scream with frustration. The masseuse's elbow dug deeper into the muscles at her neck. "Wow," the woman said. "I thought I'd loosened these babies up for good. I was wrong."

"Sorry," Maggie said, projecting her voice so it could be heard past the donut her head was in. "I think I'm about to undo a lot of your work right now."

She heard Bugs groan. "You don't need to yell at me right now. You can yell at me later. I hear couples like yelling at each other in a car."

Maggie gripped the vinyl of the donut. She could swear her nails were slicing into the thing. She tried to loosen her grip as she tried to focus on the sound of the bamboo flute playing on an iPod in the corner. She tried to envision the two women in khaki shorts and white polos working on her naked back and a half-naked Bugs.

Four people are in this teeny, tiny dark room. Now is not the time. There was no hiding anything from anyone in here. She knew Bugs's masseuse was chewing grape-flavored gum and that her masseuse had allergies, the way she kept sniffing.

She could hear her mother's voice: *This is not the time, Magdalene.*

Maggie knew it wasn't the right time. She let Bugs off the hook.

For about five seconds.

"Why did you name a month?" she demanded.

She heard the sigh. "So we aren't going to let this go."

"Answer the question, Bugs."

She lifted her head. Bugs had his towel down to his waist, and his masseuse was working on his shoulders.

The man had awesome shoulders. Thick muscles were everywhere she looked: shoulders, biceps, even his back.

How did this science nerd have this body? The question distracted her from why she started this inquisition in the first place.

"Are you really a bug guy?" she asked, resting her weight on an elbow, her body turned toward him, just her bra in place. Her masseuse grabbed a tissue while Maggie talked.

"Yes. I like bugs."

"And you workout?"

"I exercise."

Potato, potahto. "And you have a Ph.D.?" she asked.

"Yes."

"And Dotty said you also have an M.D.?"

"Yep." She didn't hear him sigh, but she could feel another one coming on.

She continued looking and appreciating the lay of the land that was Augustus Sloane's body. When her brain started thinking less about his body and more about his mouth, she brought herself back to reality. "Why did you tell them February?"

"I said the wedding was in February because it's winter in New Hampshire. No one visits in February."

"What does that have to do with anything?"

The long-awaited sigh finally came. "Your pretense can continue. No one will know you didn't marry anyone. You can just say you did."

She closed her eyes. Her head hurt. "Why couldn't I just say we broke up?"

"Because then the cycle would continue. You would need to rent someone else when your family visits the next time. This way, you don't need to worry about it."

"I don't need to worry?" For all the degrees and brain cells this guy had, she was starting to doubt Bug's overall intelligence. "I don't have to worry about pulling a husband out of thin air when they come? Because that sounds a whole heck of a lot harder than a fiancé. A husband lives with me. Has clothes in the closet, toothpaste in the sink, dirty cereal bowls on the kitchen table."

Bugs finally lifted his head out of his own donut. His eyes fell to her boobs, where they were just in a bra and looking directly at him. He dragged his eyes up and away. "What kind of slob do you think I am?"

"Are you saying you want the role?" Maggie found that she had forgotten how to swallow.

"You won't have to bring me up to speed. If you need an obedient, no-strings-attached hubby, call me." He shifted and put his face back into his donut hole.

Maggie's rubbed her stomach. It was better, but the butterflies that had suddenly hatched there were making her…fluttery. *Call me.*

"Or call Dotty. She can rent you someone who'll be just as good."

She stopped rubbing her tummy.

The butterflies were all dead.

Chapter Twenty-Three

"DID YOU HAVE FUN, LALA?"

It was late afternoon and Maggie sat with Roxy in the Jeep waiting for Bugs to stop talking to one of the hotel's gardeners. The day still officially Mother's Day, but to Maggie it was done and over.

Maggie had gotten quality time with Roxie building fairy houses in the hotel's courtyard. She had even spent time with her own mother, sitting in the lobby with her, Peyton and Lauren, pretending to listen as they talked about people Maggie didn't know.

"I loooooved this weekend," Roxie was saying. "I loved seeing all my cousins and playing with them, even the mean ones."

"I'm glad," Maggie said. Everyone but her mother had already taken off, and the three women had promised each other they really needed to Skype more often.

Meaning they would continue not Skyping at all, for the sake of everyone's mental health.

Maggie looked around for Bugs, who was now squatting by one of the barrels of flowers that lined the white gravel path to The Montgomery's double turquoise doors. Which was where her mother stood, staring out at the ocean. The day's breeze ruffled the hem of her skirt but not a strand of hair on her head.

Maggie guessed Aqua Net. She had first started using it back in the 1980s, when she had found work as a stemware designer. And apparently, thirty years later, she was still loyal to the stuff.

"Hey Mom."

Abigail looked at Maggie. But nothing was there. No happiness, no anger…nothing but the turquoise in her eyes. The turquoise that made up Maggie's right eye.

"Mom?"

Her mother blinked and seemed to come back to the present. Maggie could tell because the corner of her mouth curved in the smallest bit.

Maggie knew that expression too well. She and her sisters had always called in The Grimace of Giving Grief.

"How was Anne's other grandmother?" And the grief had begun.

"Roxie's grandmother is doing well. Pretty spry for 79."

"Why is she so old?"

"Being alive for 79 years does that to a person."

Her mother's grimace showed that she did not like that response. "I hope she enjoyed having you both during my weekend?"

"*Your* weekend?" Maggie stopped herself from going down that path. Instead, she kept the conversation in neutral territory. "She was glad to see Roxie. Definitely."

"Good." The way her mother said the word made Maggie think that her mother said it with a different definition in mind.

The wood steps behind Maggie creaked. "You ready to get back Maple Woods, Curly?" Augustus asked.

She nodded but didn't turn around to look at Bugs. "I have to prep for a party I'm throwing tonight," she explained to her mom.

"Oh?" Her mother sounded like she was the slightest bit interested. "An art gallery opening? A corporate fête?"

"A birthday celebration," Maggie said, purposely vague.

"Oh, that sounds nice." Abigail's grimace lightened up. In fact, it was almost gone.

But Bugs didn't get the hint. "Pajamas and perfume, right Curly? The girls are going to love it, Abigail."

The grimace returned full force, even worse than before. "Oh. It's a *child's* party."

"It's for a little girl whose family owns the largest supermarket in town," Maggie said. *Stop it. Stop it right now. You sound like you're defending yourself! You love your work. It's fun and it's fulfilling and it fits with a single mom's schedule.*

Her mother's face didn't change. Even when Roxie threw herself at her, she kept The Grimace of Giving Grief while she hugged her granddaughter. "You be a good girl, Anne."

And out of all of them, it was Roxie who showed how one should behave in such a situation.

"Grand, it's Roxie. Or Rox. Mom even likes calling me

LaLa because I like the Smurfs so much. You know. Because of that song they sing. La, la, la, la, la, laaaa, la, la, la, la, la." She danced in her Grand's arms as she did one of her favorite things: pretended she was a Smurf. "You can call me one of those names, Grand. I like any of them. Just not Anne."

Roxie's words were like magic. The Grimace evaporated, and Abigail even chuckled. "One of my role models was a woman named Coco," she said, hugging Roxie to her, smoothing her hair back from her face. "It only stands to reason that one of my favorite little girls in the world is called LaLa."

Chapter Twenty-Four

AUGUSTUS PUT THE CAR INTO PARK as Maggie pushed at a chunk of red hair stuck under the neckline of her jacket. He liked her hair. And he sort of liked her personality.

It had a way of working itself under his skin, much like a female jigger flea laying its eggs.

Maggie had a dedication to her kid and to her life that his students were still trying to find. Hell, that most of his colleagues were still trying to find.

But she was also someone who would take a lot of energy and care to keep happy.

He didn't have the time or the inclination to be that guy.

In the backseat, Roxie opened her door. "Bye Bugs."

"Bye kid."

The door slammed. Maggie stayed stayed where she was, her heterochromic eyes following Roxie as she stepped onto the sidewalk.

Curly opened her mouth, made a sound, but then that was it. But she still sat there. Like she was waiting for him to say something.

He didn't really have anything *to* say. It was 4 p.m. and a Sunday and next week was finals. The tests he gave had been made a decade ago, and came from a pool of a five-hundred questions. He chose fifty questions, a different fifty each semester, and a new essay question. His students took the test, and his three TAs graded them and recorded them.

As of today, his workload was pretty much done for the semester.

Except his life's work. He had maybe three weeks of intense analysis and extrapolation ahead of him. Three weeks of single-minded concentration.

His mind was actually partially back in his lab right now.

"Well, thanks," she said.

"You're welcome."

"Are you going to ask me what I'm thanking you for?"

That made him tune back in. "I think I know what you're thanking me for."

"Tell me."

"For posing as your fiancé this weekend."

"Why would I thank a guy that I paid for? You worked for *me*."

"Would you not thank a pizza boy who delivered your pizza?"

She raised an eyebrow. "Sure."

"Think of me as that pizza boy. I delivered a product in the time required." His debt was repaid to his aunts, too. Maybe that's what made him feel extra cocky as he said, "In fact, a pizza boy would receive a tip."

"A tip?!"

The screech made Augustus's ears ring. "I was joking, Maggie."

"Five hundred dollars for fewer than two days of service and--"

He reached out and grabbed her hand. Her fingers were like stone, they were so cold and stiff. "Relax, Curly. I already told you that I wasn't the one who took your money." In fact, it was the one issue he didn't like in this entire arrangement. He looked around. Maggie's apartment was in front of him, but next to that was The Coffee Pot. And next to that was New England Credit Union. "If you have a minute, I'll reimburse you that money."

"Oh no you don't."

"What?"

"Don't make this whole thing feel weird."

He laughed. "I think it's way too late to worry about that. It started being weird the minute Dotty came to my class and told me I was spoken for this weekend."

She didn't laugh, but she did smile, and some of the starch left her back and shoulders. It made him relax. He didn't even know he had been tense until then.

"Why would it be weird, Maggie?" His hand still held hers. He was in no rush to let it go.

She looked at her phone. "I better go. I have to set up that birthday party. Make sure the cake's been delivered. Double check each gift bag again."

"You will in a second. First, tell me why it would be weird if I gave you back the money."

She blew out a breath. "Then this wouldn't have been

business. This would have been *something*."

"Why can't it be a friend something?"

"A friend that kissed another friend something?" She shook her head. "That turns it into a big something if we take away the boundaries."

"The boundaries?"

"The payment. That made our boundaries. That kept us…"

"Strangers?"

She gave him a look. It included her family's genetically shared eyebrow arch. "No."

"Safe?"

"Maybe."

Classical music started playing. Mozart? It was coming from Maggie's phone.

She picked it up and looked at the screen. She grinned.

"Definitely not your mother or your sisters. Or your ex." Augustus studied her face. "Is it a suitor, Maggie? You have a look on your face like it's a fellow intent on courting you."

"Maybe."

"Why didn't you ask him to escort you this weekend?"

"I just met him on Friday. And he's definitely not…safe."

"Who is it?"

They sat there for minute, Maggie reading her text, him already losing interest. His lab and his work were waiting for him.

Then she said, "Noah Fisher.

Augustus kept himself from rolling his eyes. He knew Noah had texted her, but he didn't think it was turning into something.

Noah. He had to keep from snorting. The guy was a third grade teacher at Abenaki Elementary and enjoyed khakis and plaid shirts and silver hoop earrings when he was off duty.

Women liked Noah. Lots of women.

He opened his mouth, his thoughts about Noah right there, ready to share.

But Maggie had a big smile on her face, the tired look that had been there most of the weekend giving way to happy excitement.

He shut his mouth and let her have her moment. "Will you be going to the doctor about that stomach thing?"

"It's on the list," she said with a nod. But he had a feeling that list was a mile long. And going to the doctor was dead last.

Instead, he turned his attention to Roxie as she pet a golden retriever tied outside The Coffee Pot. "Do you want her petting that dog?"

Maggie looked around him and found Roxie. "She's a good judge of dogs. And people. And we met Rusty when we moved in. He's good people."

He looked for the dog's owner. "Who's Rusty?"

"The dog."

"Oh." He didn't get that. He didn't think of a dog as a person. "So what did Roxie think about me?"

"I don't know yet. You've sorta been around all weekend. You cramped our style." She started typing on her phone.

To dumbass Noah Fisher.

Not your problem, he told himself.

He looked one more time at the bank next to the coffee shop. "Are you absolutely certain I can't give you that money back? I'm sure you could--"

"Don't. You. Dare."

Augustus didn't like feeling this way. Like he should be returning her money yet couldn't. He didn't need it. She did. Roxie did.

"Can I take you both out to dinner this week?"

That made her look up. "Bugs. Did you fall in love with me?"

She was smiling. He let himself take the cue and said, "Yes, yes I did."

"No dinner. That's too…strings attached."

"You're probably going out with Noah Fisher, aren't you?"

"Maybe. But I don't know him. Dinner with him wouldn't feel like there were strings. I know you now." She gathered her purse and opened her car door. "There might be strings."

Strings. He was starting to hate that word. He looked over at Roxie, still petting the dog. "Do you need me to watch Roxie while you're at the birthday party?"

"She's my helper. The six-year-olds will love her."

So this was it. The end of their time together.

She had Noah Fisher.

He had his work.

There was nothing else to say. It was time to go.

The weekend was officially over.

"You have me until midnight." Well, he'd blurted that one out.

Her eyes widened a bit. "I do, don't I." She looked at him but wasn't *looking* at him. She appeared to be thinking. "Could you babysit Rox when I get back? I have to still workout, and so I'll need you probably from ten to eleven."

"Do you have any good snacks?"

"Cupcake-flavored Goldfish. Those packages with the processed cheese, crackers, and red sticks."

"Sold." He handed her car keys back to her as he opened the door. "See you in a few hours." And then before he closed the door, he added, "Happy Mother's Day, Curly."

Her odd but striking blue eye and green eye stared straight into his, sparking with annoyance and humor. "You're killing me with that Curly crap."

"I'll stop calling you Curly if you stop calling me Bugs."

The smile came fully out. Impossibly wide. "Never."

The End

Wow. Is that it? Really? For now it is. *Bad Mom Rents a Man: Class Reunion (Book 2)* comes out Summer 2014. Make sure to check it out when it does. If you'd like a reminder when it comes out, sign up for

The Always Awesome & Fun Newsletter

found on my website: www.sydneystrand.com.

The Author

Sydney Strand lives in Colonial America in a place where you can hear the university clock tower chime the hour and the Amtrak train whistle through town. It's a lovely existence.

She has never rented a man. But if she did, she hopes that she would have gotten a man like Bugs. He seems pretty awesome.

She loves hearing from her readers. Loves, loves, loves!

Acknowledgements

A writer is only as good as the people she surrounds herself with. This includes:

Critical Critique Partners
Brainstorming Alpha Readers
Nitpicky Beta Readers
Anal Retentive Editors
Helpful Husbands
Inspiring Children

So thank you, Shelley Coriell, Stacey Goitia, Susan Lanier Graham, Margaret Turner, Susan Stehle, Le Husband, La Petite Adult, and Le Boy Bebe.

And of course none of this would be possible without those two humans that gave me life: Mom, who was a reading specialist and had the most magical of classrooms: it was stocked with what felt like thousands of comic books (and I read them all—*Blondie, Beetle Bailey, Archie*). And Dad, who would take me to The Book Nook or The Little Professor and we'd browse for what felt like hours. My gregarious dad taught me that talking to a bookshop owner (a fellow book lover!) is one of the best people to talk to in the world

Pajamas! Kid's **PARTY** **Perfume!**

Venue!

Find a place where pajamas would be a fun choice. A large hotel room would be one option. For the more budget-minded, a large living room works, an early-morning backyard, or even a nearby group-friendly park. Do keep in mind you'll be working with smelly things, so stay away from places where others' noses may be offended (such as a children's museum or humane society).

Food!

It's a pajama party, so breakfast foods work well. Pancakes, individual cereals, donut holes, fruit, OJ. Or you can go the French route because of the perfume angle. Croissants, crepes, and tarts would work (and still be breakfast foods!).

Games!

1) Guess that scent! Find items lying around your house (candles in simple scents such as pumpkin and cranberry and extracts such as almond, peppermint, vanilla) for the children to guess with. Have a bowl of coffee beans near to help "freshen up" their ability to smell.

2) Name that scent! Have guests come up with fun names for concoctions. For instance, a blend of cranberry, pumpkin, and vanilla might be called "One Night in November."

3) Design Your Own Pajamas/Pillowcases! Print out the outline of pajamas on a white sheet of paper and have children design their own PJs! Or, if you have more money budgeted, buy each child a white pillowcase to decorate.

If you want more ideas, visit *sydneystrand*'s Pinterest page:
www.pinterest.com/sydneystrand